PROMISES TO KEEP

By Susan Lovell

Published by
KRisSCroSS Press
Grand Rapids, Michigan.

Cover design and composition by Brad Hineline.
Editorial proofing by Terry McCarthy and Diane Johnson.

Special recognition to my two expert consultants
Joyce Jensen and Daniel Irwin.

ISBN 979-8-5515815-2-9

Dedicated to Joshua who will always be twelve years old…
…and to his loving family.

ABOUT THE AUTHOR

SUSAN LOVELL is the prize-winning author of *The Sandpiper* and its sequel *Behold A Rainbow*, now published by Amazon on Kindle. Lovell started *Cadence*, a weekly newspaper in East Grand Rapids, Michigan, and has written four non-fiction books, including the **History of The Wege Foundation** about the founder of Steelcase, Inc. With honors undergraduate and graduate degrees from the University of Michigan, Lovell has served on the boards of the Salvation Army and Our Hope, both in their recovery programs.

STOPPING BY WOODS ON A SNOWING EVENING

By Robert Frost

Whose woods these are I think I know.
His house is in the village though;
He will not see me stopping here
To watch his woods fill up with snow.

My little horse must think it queer
To stop without a farmhouse near
Between the woods and frozen lake
The darkest evening of the year.

He gives his harness bells a shake
To ask if there is some mistake.
The only other sound's the sweep
Of easy wind and downy flake.

The woods are lovely, dark and deep,
But I have promises to keep,
And miles to go before I sleep,
And miles to go before I sleep.

PROMISES TO KEEP

FRIDAY NOVEMBER 19, 2010

Dear God, help me, Jamie Cameron prayed out loud to her image in the bathroom mirror as she gripped the cell phone in her hand. *Please, God, tell me he didn't just say that…that word.* Jamie dropped the phone on the counter as she leaned against it to keep herself steady. She needed a drink. Then she shook her head hard enough to hurt. Alcoholics don't ever ever *need* a drink. She knew better. I *want* a drink.

Over two years of hard-worked recovery, daily AA meetings, reading the Big Book, doing the 12 steps with her tough sponsor Gloria—yet right now Jamie's guts clenched with cravings as if she'd never been sober. She kept her two-year AA coin tucked behind her driver's license and really believed she had finally overcome that impulsive first drink.

But Keith had just called—and like a snake coiled in her brain, the craving leaped up. As if it had just been waiting for a chance to strike. One word, one word over the phone was all it took. Jamie wondered if Orwell's rat torture was like this. Her head felt like Winston's must have locked in a cage, rats screeching next to his face. Jamie had hated *1984* when she'd read it in high school. She'd despised Winston for making Julia take his place and let the rats eat her face instead of his.

But right now she was Winston. Ready to sacrifice all the people she loved most in the world for one drink. Just one drink so she didn't have to think about why Keith had called. Knowing that first drink would never be enough and she'd hurt the people she loved most in the world. Her daughter Minka. Her mother Ellie and her sister Kate. And Maddie—the bright young woman Jamie had rescued from a mentally ill, abusive mother. Jamie made herself see

1

their faces in her head. One drink would break all their hearts.

She thought of the note Aunt Nina had written in the anthology she'd given Jamie just before she died. Nina had written notes next to some of the poems. Jamie could visualize the familiar handwriting next to Tennyson's "Crossing the Bar." Aunt Nina's double entendre on the sand *bar* to Jamie. "… and may there be no moaning of the bar when I put out to sea."

'Do not use my death as an excuse to head to a bar,' Aunt Nina had written. Aunt Nina was telling Jamie that no grief, no troubles, no stress ever justified a drink. That meant never! It meant Keith's one word today did not justify a drink. No matter how terrified Jamie was about why he needed to talk to her alone.

'I want to take Minka out for lunch next Friday,' he'd called this morning to say as Jamie was putting on her makeup. Fine, she'd quickly agreed. 'You two need time together before you leave for Arizona.' But then Keith went on. After lunch, he wanted to have a conversation with Jamie alone.

'What about, Keith?' she'd asked innocently. When he didn't answer right away, she asked again, her tone no longer easy, 'Why can't you tell me now!'

Then came the word that had knocked the breath out of Jamie. 'Custody.' The father Minka hadn't known until she was four? The man Jamie'd had a 'one-night-stand' with wanted to talk about custody?

Jamie took some deep yoga breaths and started to obsess on the small pill bottle hidden in a Tampax box under the bathroom sink. 'Custody.' Minka's father with the perfect life had said it. The famous therapist and bestselling author, Dr. Keith Summers wanted to talk about custody with Minka's mother, the recovering alcoholic.

One small Antabuse would short circuit the bite her brain was demanding. Drinking on top of Antabuse would make her sick enough to die. That's why she kept the pills, she reassured herself. For an emergency. Today was one.

But then her AA sponsor Gloria Cook's brown face floated up. Nobody had a more loving heart than this devout deacon of the Good Shepherd Baptist Church. But neither was anyone more hard-core than Gloria about the 12 Steps.

'Oh,' Jamie could hear Gloria saying in her commanding voice. 'So the father of your daughter, who by the way is *not* your husband, might want to share custody with *your* daughter because Minka is *his* daughter too?' Jamie could just picture the anger on Gloria's face as she shook her head crowned with rich sable curls.

'So now, girlfriend,' Gloria would point an angry finger at Jamie, 'you got yourself an excuse to drink! Pull out your old pity pot and let 'er rip.' Just imagining Gloria's reaction, Jamie felt her face heat up in shame. To Gloria Antabuse was an alcoholic's crutch. And after Jamie's last relapse two years before, Gloria hadn't asked, but ordered–as she always did–Jamie to never take one of those pills again.

Jamie studied her face in the mirror as she brushed her long blond hair. That she was 42 didn't stop men at the club from calling her 'hot' making sure she could hear them. Still the lean athlete she'd been as a champion swimmer and elite downhill skier, she knew what they wanted. They were 13th Steppers, men with enough sobriety to hit on women who were AA newcomers. Even after two years, they still zeroed in on Jamie. Fellow alcoholics, they knew how vulnerable she still was.

Jamie yanked her hair into a ponytail, pulling hard enough to cause pain as if that might stop the cravings. She saw her eyes wince, the eyes Aunt Nina called "Aegean" blue–Nina Judd loved Greek mythology. Jamie's sister Kate had inherited their dad's dark eyes. Jamie Cameron had inherited his name– the dad she'd never met.

Dr. James Cameron, the war hero who'd volunteered for Vietnam. He'd grown increasingly outraged by the long-haired hippies who couldn't be drafted out of the University of Michigan. Jim Cameron knew other young men who could not afford college were coming home in body bags.

One May day James Cameron was walking across the Diag on the center of Michigan's campus when one of the anti-war marchers lit up his draft card. The new Dr. Cameron hit a breaking point. He heard a satisfying grunt as he smashed his farm-hardened fist directly into the card burner's gut exactly where he knew from studying anatomy it would hurt the most.

That afternoon Dr. Cameron went to the draft board in Washtenaw County without telling his wife Ellie–whose love for her husband bordered on worship. Jim Cameron was the man Ellie couldn't live without. But then one day the soldiers came to the door of the Sandpiper's log cabin–and Ellie descended into blackness.

On impulse, like a typical alcoholic, Jamie dug out the pill bottle and swallowed an Antabuse. Now if she relapsed, she could die. "Sorry, Gloria," she said out loud as she raised her water glass to the mirror. Then her mind went back to Dr. Keith Summer's office in the Tucson women's rehab where he'd agreed to see his patient on a Sunday as an emergency. She had needed to talk to him.

But then Jamie, who knew better than anyone how easily men were seduced, made a move that changed everything. Jamie quickly put on her insulated running clothes and headed out the door. She couldn't exorcise her fears with alcohol now, so a long hard run in the cold wind had to do it. Minka wouldn't be home from school for hours. She just might have to run until then.

THURSDAY JULY 1, 2010

The sound of waves helped calm Minka as she pedaled south down the dirt road where she'd been heading more and more lately. It was an area called The Dunes where the cottages were bigger and farther apart. She could think better with no cars driving around. Pogo loped beside her, his tail wagging as always on these walks. If only she could be happy like her dear old Pogo, the Cameron family's dog, the stray who'd saved her mother's life.

Minka couldn't stop thinking about her dad's moving to Arizona, so far away. She thought about how happy she'd been the day she met him. She was only four, but still remembered feeling like the luckiest girl on Earth to have a dad. A real dad. And such a nice one. He lived in Chicago but drove to Spring Port on the west side of Michigan almost every weekend to see her.

In the summers she loved kayaking with him up and down the Lake Michigan shoreline for hours at a time. They would do it this Sunday on the Fourth and watch the fireworks from the water like they did every year. The last few winters he'd taken her up north skiing. But she was still not really used to calling him, 'Dad' so she tended to refer to him as 'my dad.'

He often brought her a present. For her seventh birthday he'd given her the American Girl doll Kaya she'd picked out from the catalog. She wanted Kaya because she was from the Nez Perce tribe and Minka knew they were the ones who named the lake she lived on 'Michigan.' It came from the Ojibwe's word 'mishigami' meaning 'big water.'

Her dad's girlfriend Pat had come with her dad the last few years and Minka liked her. Everyone in the family did. But Minka had still hoped her dad would marry her mom so the three of them could be a family and live together.

Then in early June her dad suddenly announced he was accepting a new job as the CEO of the rehab hospital in Tucson called Saguaro where her mom had been in treatment and he'd been the psychiatrist. Pat was going with him. Last weekend her dad brought Minka a tourist book on Tucson with beautiful photographs of the Sonoran desert–the mountains behind the giant cactuses and the wildflowers in bloom. 'And it's warm and sunny all winter,' he'd said.

But Minka knew how far away Tucson was. It would be like losing him all over again. And now if Pat was going with him, Minka's prayer would never come true. She blinked her eyelids as hard as she could. Almost from the day she'd found out Dr. Summers was her real dad, Minka's prayer every night was the same. "Dear God, please let my mom and dad get married." Sometimes she'd bargain with Him.

"I'll never drink." That would be easy after watching her mother. "I'll get all As." That was doable too. Her most recent trade offer was not to eavesdrop anymore. That, however, would be hard to keep. It was the only way she knew what was going to happen with her dad moving away.

All at once she heard nearby flute music. Maddie sometimes practiced the flute she had played in the Spring Port High School band. Pogo must have thought it was Maddie because he turned down a narrow dirt road through blowing beach grass and ran toward the music. Minka pointed her handlebars after him riding up a dune to see an enormous white cottage where someone in a wheelchair on the back deck was playing the flute.

The music abruptly stopped and Minka heard a young woman's voice say, "Well, hello you," to Pogo. Minka now saw it was a girl who looked a few years older than she was in the wheelchair. "What a lovely dog you have," the girl said to Minka in a soft breathlessness. "What's his, or her, name?"

"He's Pogo. A boy. I'm Minka Cameron."

"I'm Andrea Armitage," Minka heard the wheezing as she spoke. "And I can't tell you how happy I am to meet you, Minka. I'm just here for the summer and don't know anyone my age. I don't look it but I am 17. And you are how old? Please, come sit by me," she motioned to the blue webbed chair beside her.

"I'll be twelve in November," Minka said. "But I did skip a grade so I'm a year ahead in school if that counts."

"Then I say you are at least twelve because you must be smart and I think you're as tall as I am if I were standing up. And you do look older than eleven," Andrea took a deep breath. She twirled the flute in one hand while she spoke.

"They make me play this so my lungs will work harder," she tapped her chest with the flute. "Thank you for giving me an excuse to stop."

Minka slid the chair closer to Andrea before she sat down. Then she couldn't help staring. Andrea had the palest skin she'd ever seen. Andrea's face gave Minka the impression she could see the blood moving through her veins.

The arresting blue of her eyes shone even bluer against her white cheeks. Her hair was a shiny auburn cut short with thick bangs straight across her forehead. And hot as it was, Andrea wore a purple Northwestern sweatshirt and Bermuda shorts. When Minka saw her swollen knees and ankles, she guessed that was why Andrea was in the wheelchair. At her neck glinted a small gold cross. A barely visible line of sweat at her temples made Minka wonder if just playing the flute was hard work for her.

Then Andrea smiled. And before she could stop herself, Minka blurted, "You've got a space too!" and touched the gap between her own two front teeth!

"Yes, I do!" Andrea exclaimed as her face miraculously flushed with vigor. "Can you spit water between yours?" Andrea asked and mimicked the maneuver with her tongue pressed against the back of her two front teeth.

Then Andrea reached over with one hand, and as Minka took it into hers, she felt an almost spiritual connection. Like they'd known each other before. Minka knew it wasn't true. But in that moment, their invisible bond felt more real to her than the wooden deck underneath them.

It never mattered again that Andrea was older and sickly. Minka was living with such anxiety about losing her dad that Andrea's simple pureness was a balm to her heart. Pogo seemed to feel it too as he sat upright in front of the wheelchair with his big head on Andrea's slender lap.

Minka had never met anyone, young or old, who gave her such a sense of peace. Andrea's almost musical voice, her graceful hand gestures, her way of looking into Minka's eyes made Andrea seem almost otherworldly. Like an angel even.

"Can I tell you a secret?" Minka surprised herself by asking.

Andrea turned the wheels on her chair toward Minka so they could face each other straight on. "Well, yes. But only if I can tell you mine," Andrea stared into Minka's eyes.

For the first time since her dad had said he was moving, Minka felt calm. Calmer here with Andrea than anywhere else.

"It's about my dad. I didn't know him until I was four because my mom refused to talk about him. It was like he was dead. My Uncle Pete and my friend Tommy's dad Uncle Joe tried to be like dads to me, but...," Minka paused.

"...they weren't your dad and it's not the same," Andrea finished the sentence.

Minka pulled on her thick brown ponytail as she nodded in gratitude. It felt like Andrea was easing a load on her back she hadn't realized weighed so much. Deep inside Minka felt a warmth. An unexpected sense of security. Here was someone outside her family who could understand. And not judge. And above all, not tell anyone anything Minka said.

Minka began talking faster. "I know my mom met him at the same rehab clinic he's going to take over in Tucson and I know..." then she paused. "Well, they had sex because I was born six months after she left rehab in April. I *can* count to nine, Andrea!"

Andrea made a rolling little giggle and nodded her head.

"And just so you know I found out about sex when I was really young and my Aunt Kate and Uncle Pete were having twins. Everyone was so weird about it when I was around. They kept changing the subject if the pregnancy came up.

"So my friend Maddie–who's more like an older sister–explained it to me. She was in college then and said she'd want to know too. She also told me the twins were in vitro babies and explained that to me too. I'm known for asking too many questions, and Maddie knew I'd want the whole story."

"Wow!" Andrea said. "That's so cool. You're the first person I've ever known who has family with in vitro babies."

Minka couldn't believe how easy it was to talk about this with an older girl she'd just met. Then Minka pulled her chair closer to the wheelchair. "Now the only thing they've said to me about my dad's new job is that they're sorry he won't be able to visit weekends. But what they don't know is he wants me to move with him to Tucson. Last weekend he brought me this fancy tourist book on Arizona with all these great colored photos. I hid it in my room so Mom wouldn't see it."

"Because she'd know why he gave it to you and get worried," Andrea said.

Minka felt her eyes start to sting. "How come you say the words I'm afraid to, Andrea?"

Andrea reached again for Minka's hand. "I'm sure talking about how in vitro works is far easier for you, Minka, than telling me this about your dad,"

Andrea said gently.

Minka didn't say anything. Andrea had just spoken for her again.

"My mom had a drinking problem before I was born," Minka began to run out words as fast as she could. Like a dam bursting. "That's why she was in a rehab hospital in Tucson," Minka continued her speed monologue.

"My dad was her psychiatrist there–that's where they had their affair. Now my dad's going back to be the chief executive at Saguaro, that's the rehab's name." She didn't give Andrea time to respond. Minka had to get this all out now.

"My mom left Saguaro early to take care of Aunt Nina, my grandmother's best friend, who was dying of cancer. Her real name was Helena, but everyone called her Nina, and I'm named Helena for her. Minka is the name my friend Tommy gave me when he couldn't say 'Helena.'" Finally she paused to take a deep breath.

"Your mom must have loved Aunt Nina very much to leave treatment early so she could take care of her, and then name you after her," Andrea said quietly.

Minka nodded silently. "She did. Everybody loved Aunt Nina. But, Andrea, what's confusing is that my mother never knew her own dad because he was killed in Vietnam before she was born. So she knows how it feels not to have a dad. And she saw that I was happier than I'd ever been to finally have a dad. But now?" Minka shook her head. "I almost wish I'd never met him."

"Oh, no, Minka," Andrea said leaning forward. "He's in your life now. That's such a gift to you."

"But he'll be so far away! We've been together almost every weekend since I was four. And now he's taught me how to ski and I love it. That won't happen anymore."

"But there's skiing in Arizona and you can go there. Plus he can still come here. My dad has a plane and flies here from Chicago in twenty minutes. I know Tucson is much farther away, but do you know how long it takes to fly there from Chicago?"

"Too long for me to go for a weekend or for him to come here because I'm in school and he'll be working."

Andrea leaned back, her face radiant from more than just the sun. "Of course you'd know that. You haven't thought about much else since you found this out, have you sweetheart."

Now Minka felt tears rolling down her face. She didn't know why she knew it, but she'd known Andrea would understand. Would care. Knew she would never tell anyone.

Andrea stroked Pogo's greying head as a soft breeze ruffled her shiny reddish brown hair. "Now I will share with you what I can't talk about with anyone else. Especially in Winnetka where we live." Andrea took a deep inhale and tapped her chest. "My friends at school wondered why I couldn't do the rock climb or the ropes in gym. My hands," she held out her swollen fingers, "couldn't grip.

"You can see my puffy joints," she said raising her legs. "I even got teased about the way I walked. But I didn't tell anyone because I didn't want them to feel sorry for me. I missed so much school I never really had any close friends or I might have told them. The teachers always knew what was wrong with me, but they also knew I didn't want anyone to pity me so they never talked about it."

Andrea's shoulders went up as she took a deep breath and leaned toward Minka. "I was diagnosed with rheumatoid arthritis when I was two. It's an autoimmune disease which means my body is attacking itself."

"I do know about that, Andrea. My Uncle Pete's niece Caroline has juvenile diabetes and that's an autoimmune disease too. My grandmother talks about arthritis in her fingers, but I never heard the word rheumatoid." Minka was getting a bad feeling in her stomach.

"You're right on all counts, my smart new friend. Your uncle's niece's Type One Diabetes attacks her own pancreas while your grandmother's arthritis happens pretty much to everybody as they get older and their joints stiffen. Rheumatoid arthritis is different. It can happen at any age and attacks the lining of joints." Andrea pointed at the swollen knuckles on the other hand.

Instinctively Minka began circling her soft fingers over the red knobs of knuckle bone on Andrea's hand. "Oh, my," Andrea purred. "You are now my best friend forever. Heat and ice don't work, but your tickles do."

Minka knew it wasn't really true, but she kept on moving back and forth over both of Andrea's sore hands wanting to absorb the pain into her own fingers.

"Is that your secret?" Minka asked without looking up from her massaging. "Rheumatoid arthritis?"

Andrea paused, looking around to make sure they were still alone. "No. I've been in and out of hospitals and doctors' offices since I was two so, no. That's just to explain what my secret really is.

"Because of what's happened to my immune system, my breathing is getting worse. You can hear me wheezing, can't you?"

Andrea raised her eyebrows waiting for a response.

Minka nodded her head slowly. "I heard it as soon as you started talking."

"Minka, here is my secret. I'm sharing only with you." Andrea took a deep audible breath as if to prove what she was going to say. "I now have Autoimmune Bronchiolitis Obliterans and it can't be cured."

"NO!" Minka almost shouted squeezing both Andrea's hands. "NO!"

"Shh," Andrea said nodding toward the cottage behind her. "My parents and Nana, my grandmother, don't think I know. Well, I think my dad knows I do, but he's protecting my mother. She's been in a sort of denial about my disease all along.

"That's the other part of my secret, Minka. At an appointment with one of my many doctors–this one was my lung specialist–in May, the nurse left my file where she'd been sitting when she got beeped away." Andrea half smiled at Minka. "I am sure you are nosey too and would have done the same thing."

Minka nodded biting on her lower lip as her eyes burned. "So I opened it and read as fast as I could. The hand written diagnosis note was a term I hadn't seen before so I memorized it fast. I had the folder closed back on the chair when the nurse returned. But my heart was beating so fast I knew my face was red. And she noticed.

"She asked me if I was OK, and I found out what a good liar I can be. I told her I'd just been doing my deep breathing exercises and they always make my face flush. She trusted me so much I felt guilty."

"But you had to, Andrea," Minka said with passion. "And, yes, I am nosey too. The only reason I know what they say about my dad's moving is because I eavesdrop on Mom and Elliegram whenever I can. I have a hiding place in the Sandpiper cottage where my grandmother Ellie and her husband Casey live just up a little hill from the log cabin where my mom and I live. That's the only way I would ever know what's going on! Your parents don't tell you everything either I guess."

Minka and Andrea sat quietly together watching a pair of seagulls hover low over the blowing beach grass along the dirt road. "I've never told anyone that, Minka. The past two months I've had to pretend with my parents and Nana that my new shortness of breath will get better in this clean Lake Michigan air."

Minka began to tremble, and grabbed Andrea's forearm. Feeling the bones under the thick sweatshirt made her cry harder. "How can it be that I love you already, Andrea, and can't stand to hear this from you? You're the only person I can trust now. You have to get better!"

Andrea's pale skin seemed to almost glow as she laid her hand over Minka's. "My sweet Minka. I believe God puts the very people in our lives we need the most just when we need them most. Why else was I playing the flute when you rode down our road with this goofy dog who won't take his head off my lap? You and I woke up this morning with secrets breaking our hearts.

"And now," she leaned toward Minka and looked straight into her eyes, "we each have a best friend we can talk to about it. I mean, really, don't you just feel better that I know about your mom and dad? Because I feel an enormous relief telling you about me. Honestly, you're going to help me do a better job of pretending—especially with my mom."

Then Andrea abruptly pulled a plastic water bottle out of the side pocket on her wheelchair. "Now I'm going to show you how sick I am not!" Minka stared in amazement as Andrea took a big breath, filled her mouth with water, leaned back and then spit a fine stream of water into the air landing just beyond the deck.

"Now," Andrea said, between big gulps of air, "try to beat that," and handed Minka the water bottle.

Minka stared at Andrea in shock as she mindlessly took the bottle. Then she felt a surge of joy, and lifted the bottle chugging in a mouthful, opened her lips over the space between her two front teeth and tried to spit as hard as she could. But the laughter in her chest had to come out and she collapsed in her chair, water dripping down her chin, before she could empty her mouth on the deck.

"Winner winner chicken dinner! " Andrea called out raising her hands in triumph.

"Well, I never," both girls turned toward the grey-haired woman in a blue silk dress wearing a long string of pearls. "I'm Andrea's grandmother Nana and her mother and I were so happy to see she had a friend out here, we just stayed inside. But all that laughter! So good to hear our girl having fun," she patted Andrea's head, a big diamond ring on her finger shooting fire from the sunlight.

"What fun conversations you two must be having."

Minka and Andrea exchanged glances. And then they couldn't hold back. Side by side under the clear blue sky, they broke down in shoulder-shaking laughs that filled the world around them.

TWO P.M. SATURDAY, NOVEMBER 20, 2010

Jamie pulled the chain to open the vertical blinds on her first-floor office window that were usually closed for her counseling clients' privacy. But today she was here to make a phone call that needed quiet, but not drawn blinds.

Rolling her desk chair forward, Jamie did what she always did in her office to gear up for a patient–especially on the days she was seeing one of her too many teenagers stuck in the dark place of addiction. Jamie pulled out the anthology Aunt Nina had left her. For Jamie it felt almost like a prayer asking for her wisdom to help the troubled young soul she was waiting for. But today it was not to gear up for a client. But for a phone call.

And she always looked for a page with Aunt Nina's familiar scrawl on it. Yesterday Jamie had drawn on Aunt Nina's note beside Tennyson's *Crossing the Bar* to fight off a relapse. Only Nina would have turned Tennyson's sandbar into a tavern! No, even though her beloved Aunt Nina had died nine years before, she would never be out of Jamie's life. Aunt Nina had made sure of that.

Tennyson's "No moaning of the bar when I put out to sea" was still in Jamie's head as she riffled pages for another note from Nina. Then a huge smiley face caught her eye. It was next to a quote by Polonius in *Hamlet* as a father's parting advice to his son Laertes setting sail for France.

This above all: to thine own self be true,
And it must follow, as the night the day,
Thou canst not then be false to any man.

Nervous as Jamie was about the call she was going to make, she had to smile at the classic Aunt Nina memory. The day Jamie had brought home an AA coin for six months of sobriety, she had taken her trophy straight into

Aunt Nina's bedroom. The cancer had stripped away Aunt Nina's once formidable supply of energy.

Aunt Nina smiled as she took the sobriety coin and read the Serenity Prayer on one side. But when Nina turned it over, Jamie could hear her smother a laugh. "This line on the back of your sobriety coin came from Polonius's speech in *Hamlet*."

"Of course you would know that, wouldn't you, Aunt Nina. But what's funny about it? *This above all to thine own self be true*," Jamie read out loud. "I don't get the joke."

"Oh, honey," Aunt Nina said in her thin voice. "Only an unreformed English teacher would think it's funny."

"O.K. Spit it out, Aunt Nina, cuz I know you want to tell me."

Aunt Nina sighed. "You know me way too well, my darling Jamie. Okay. So Shakespeare has Polonius telling his son Laertes to be 'true to thyself' knowing the audience would laugh at the hypocrisy. Throughout *Hamlet*, the audience—who by the way didn't miss much in Shakespeare's plays—had watched the old windbag Polonius deceive and manipulate, even exploit his own daughter, all for his own self-interest. It's one of Shakespeare's most ironic lines.

"But, my Jamie girl," she had held the coin up in her thin fingers, "who cares about Polonius if this quote helps one single alcoholic stay sober for one single day. And Polonius's actual words to be 'true to thyself' certainly fit the 'rigorous honesty' AA requires."

The connection to Aunt Nina had done what Jamie'd hoped. Aunt Nina had always known when Jamie needed to be pushed back and when to be lifted up. "To thine own self be true," she said laughing out loud. Now she was ready to make her call.

As she reached for the office phone, her cell rang. "Hey," Joe O'Connor said in his familiar husky voice. "Brenda said you wanted us to let Minka hang out here after the movie this afternoon."

"I hope that's not a problem," Jamie said.

"Of course not, Jamie. They have a running tally shooting hoops playing Pig. Tommy gives her a handicap shot because he's older, but I don't think he's doing that much longer. Minka's going to be a jock like you, Jamie. I've read those old news clips when you blew away the state swim meet.

"No, Jamie, I'm calling because, well, Brenda and I are kind of worried about Minka. Even Tommy says he's seen a change in her lately. Our daredevil chatterbox is just not herself. Too quiet. We think it's about Keith's moving to Arizona–but she's known that since summer."

"Your reporter skills don't miss much do they, Joe? You're more right than you can imagine." Jamie pinched her nose against tears. "It's actually why I asked Brenda if Minka could stay at your house after the movie. I need to call…"

"Stop," Joe cut in. "I do not mean to pry, Jamie. Our families are too close for that. And now I'm afraid my investigative reporter obsession with locating Minka's father has, well, backfired. I hate the thought that my finding her dad has ended up making Minka vulnerable where she wasn't before. If Minka hadn't met her dad, she wouldn't…"

"No!" Jamie blurted. "No. Neither of us would take that away from her, Joe. You and I both know Gloria would *never* have helped you find Keith if it wasn't the right thing. This is what I'm going to talk about with the family this afternoon at Mom's. About Keith and his moving to Arizona before I meet Gloria at AA. So you have Minka for dinner."

"Brenda already told her we're having the tacos she loves."

"You three have been such true friends to Minka and me, Joe. Even when I've screwed up."

"Hey. We're family too, remember? Minka and Tommy have been connected at the hip since Minka could walk. I'm going out to shoot hoops with them after the movie, and they just better not beat me. Especially your daughter! See you whenever you get here."

Jamie hung up and took some deep yoga breaths. Then she dialed her mother's number.

"Hey, Mom," Jamie said in her most chipper voice. No need to alarm anyone ahead of time. Yesterday she couldn't get herself together enough to call. She would have broken down hearing her mother's voice–and she felt like she might now. But she swallowed hard and went on. "I'm sorry to do this last minute, Mom. But I'd like to come talk to you and Casey around four today if possible. I'm calling Kate and Maddie, too, so we can have a little family confab."

"Something's wrong, isn't it, Jamie? I can hear it in your voice."

Jamie rubbed her hand over her forehead. What is it about mothers? How do they always know what hasn't yet been said. "It's about Minka and Keith, isn't it?" Ellie asked before Jamie answered the first question.

"Oh, mom," Jamie said no longer faking a cheery voice. "Yes, it is." She felt her neck tighten into spasm as she strained not to cry. "Please, would you please call Kate and Maddie for me? Minka's with Joe and Brenda until after dinner." She didn't need to wait for an answer. "Thank you, Mom. I'll be at the Sandpiper by four." Jamie put the phone down fast and laid her head on the desk, letting the tears come.

Jamie was washing her face in the office bathroom when she heard a familiar sound at the office door. Three quick hard knocks in case Jamie had a client. Maddie was outside. Jamie had first met Maddie Langston when she was a high school girl cleaning the offices in the building after hours.

Jamie'd come back to her office one evening to pick up some files when she surprised Maddie, one hand on a silent vacuum, so absorbed reading a book on the desk that she didn't hear Jamie come in. That was the beginning of their very special student-mentor relationship. When Jamie found out Maddie's father had been killed in a bar fight and her mentally ill mother was abusive, Maddie soon became family to Jamie and to all the Camerons.

Then the brilliant young Maddie solved the murder of Aunt Annie, a reclusive antiques dealer and pawnbroker Maddie had cleaned for—and cared about. The town of Spring Port was stunned to find out Aunt Annie, who was considered a misfit by the town, had accumulated a fortune selling antiques and junk.

But only those down on their luck knew that Aunt Annie quietly did pawn broking for them to help out during hard times. The biggest surprise, however, to Spring Port and to Maddie came when they found out Aunt Annie, whose real name was Anushka, had willed her entire estate to the teenager. Maddie Langston had been kind to the Russian immigrant who spoke broken English when others in town had shunned her.

Now an honors graduate in psychology from Albion with a Masters in Philanthropy and Nonprofit Leadership from Grand Valley State University, Maddie ran the Sandpiper Foundation. It had been started by Aunt Nina's investment club, and Maddie had been given the Foundation's first college scholarship.

The first thing Maddie did with her out-of-the-blue inheritance was to create a new scholarship for a deserving graduate of Spring Port High and name it for Helena Nina Judd. Aunt Nina had been the one customer who'd treated Anushka as a friend and Maddie knew she had planned to do that just before she was murdered. The next thing Maddie did with her inheritance was set up another scholarship named for Anushka. That was what Maddie wanted.

"You look like you've been crying," the dark-eyed Maddie said when Jamie opened the door. Jamie half coughed. "I was going to the say the same thing to you, Maddie. You never could hide your anxiety from me. So what's going on?" Jamie asked rolling her chair around the desk as Maddie sat down across from her.

Maddie opened both hands in surrender, accepting Jamie's observation. "But I at least don't have to ask you that question, Jamie. It has to be about Minka with Keith moving out West so soon."

Jamie half smiled. "I knew you were precocious the night I found you here," she pointed at the desk, "reading my abnormal psych book. You were already onto Alfred as a dangerous sociopath. Here I was his therapist, but you were the one who figured out he'd killed poor Aunt Annie. And you used Doestoevsky to do it! I mean what teenager is that smart?"

"That was years ago, Jamie. I'm not that smart anymore."

"We all know better Maddie. Now can you please come to the Sandpiper today at four? Mom's going to call you–but since you're here."

"I forgot my phone which is why I didn't call to say I was coming. Of course I'll be there. You know Minka's my little sister."

"As you are her big sister, Maddie. Now what's up?"

Maddie pushed the sleeves up on her Notre Dame sweatshirt, out of Aunt Nina's prized college-sweatshirts collection, as if she were going to scrub dishes. She'd done a lot of that growing up taking care of her unstable mother. Jamie recognized the gesture as Maddie's emotional sign she was gearing up to do unpleasant work.

"It's about Ben."

"The guy from high school you've been going out with? The tall dark-haired good looking dude we met at the Coast Guard Festival last summer?"

"Yes," Maddie nodded her head slowly. "The football star three years ahead of me. Remember he's the one who slammed Alfred into the lockers when he heard Alfred call me 'white trash' or 'whore child,' whatever cruel epithet he used that day. It shut Alfred up for a while because Ben was a big deal in school. All the girls had a crush on Ben–including me."

"I remember what happened, but never knew who it was. So this Ben sounds like a stand-up guy. And after Gary, you deserve a good one." Gary Brown had been Maddie's boyfriend until he got drunk and climbed on her in bed until she landed a kick in his groin.

Maddie had dialed Casey Brennan, Ellie's second husband and Spring Port's Chief of Police, when Gary hit her in the jaw. Casey heard Maddie scream before her phone crashed off.

Using the police light on his car, Casey was in Maddie's apartment fifteen minutes later, his face beet red. Everyone, including the furious Maddie, was glad Gary had left. They didn't want to think about what the big Irishman, even in his pajamas, might have done to Gary. Instead Casey called the officer on patrol who caught up with Gary and arrested him for assault and battery plus drunk driving.

"At least the Gary nightmare is over," Maddie said.

"Are you saying this is another nightmare?" Jamie asked, a new solemnity in her voice.

Maddie, whose lightly freckled face had tightened, finally looked right at her mentor and friend. "Jamie, how can you tell if someone is addicted to opioids?"

{ 4 }

Promises To Keep

WEDNESDAY JULY 28, 2010

"Now I'm going to ask you, Minka, why the myth of Perseus used to be your favorite," Andrea spoke in her soft sweet voice. Then she took in a big breath. "But first I'm going to guess why I think it is."

Today the girls were sitting in a pine-paneled room filled with bookshelves inside Andrea's expansive cottage where Minka had gotten lost the first time she tried to find the bathroom. On the soft carpet, Pogo slept soundly half way between them as if not to show favoritism.

Both girls, and especially the dog, had hoped to be outside when Minka and Pogo arrived that morning. But the winds off Lake Michigan had been too strong for Andrea's breathing, even on the back deck where the house offered some shelter. Outside the library's windows the wind continued to whistle as the whitecaps overlapped each other.

Ever since Minka brought the children's book of Greek myths from the Sandpiper not long after she'd heard Andrea playing Mozart, the two had been swapping tales about them. The gory ones like gouging out Polyphemus's only eye. And the sad love story of poor Psyche and Cupid and the unfortunate tale of Persephone kidnapped by Hades. But they both especially liked the stories about the heroes like Hector and Ulysses, Theseus and Achilles.

"If you were anyone else, Andrea," Minka finally answered, "I'd bet money you couldn't guess. But you already know me way too well and you're so smart you know everything in every Greek myth we've talked about–including from the *Iliad* and the *Odyssey!*"

"When you can't even ride your horse, you get to read a lot."

"Oh, Andrea," Minka said shaking her head. "It's just so unfair." She pointed at the framed picture on the wall of a beautiful girl with reddish brown pigtails sitting proudly on a sleek chestnut horse holding a silver trophy. "Look how awesome you are on your beautiful Ginger. How old were you here?"

"Oh, I'm sorry," Minka said when she saw her friend's eyes glisten.

"No. It's all right. The way arthritis affected my knees and hips made walking hard, but riding was something I could do. I did love it. I was ten in this picture–the last year I competed. Even riding got too painful."

Minka walked over to the photograph and read the brass plate under it. "You won for ten-and-under in Stadium Show Jumping. What is that?"

"Like an obstacle course indoors. Different sized wooden jumps. Some water to go over. Bushes. Ginger had such a good trainer in Libertyville that she did all the work and I just held the reins."

"I know that's not so, Andrea. It's one more thing that I admire about you. You don't let anything stop you. I'm just so proud to be your new best friend."

"Doesn't it feel kind of like we've always been best friends, Minka? They say eyes are the windows of the soul and the day we met, I honestly saw in your dark brown ones a compassion that filled an empty space in me."

The sound of the wind suddenly filled the room as both girls looked toward the windows to see big whitecaps rolling onto the beach in serpentine patterns of turquoise and foaming white, the mid-July sun shining sparkles on the water.

Then Andrea suddenly narrowed her brilliant blue eyes and leaned forward. "Hey! You're just trying to distract me to get out of losing a bet, you stinker!"

Minka felt her heart constrict. Andrea was the bravest person she'd ever met.

"Okay then. You just try," Minka said fast.

"It's because Perseus didn't know who his father was either," Andrea answered with unusual force for her. "And that's why his was your favorite myth before you met your own father."

"Another 'winner winner, chicken dinner,' you brainiac," Minka said laughing. "Of course I liked reading about all the amazing stuff Perseus did. Killing the Gorgon was crazy! And, yes, because he didn't know who his dad was either. But Perseus and I both knew *some* male had to have sex with our moms. And it didn't matter that Zeus was Perseus's dad. Perseus still had a right to know him even if he was a god!"

Since the day they'd met, talking about sex was no different to Minka and

Andrea than talking about the Blackhawks and the Redwings, their favorite hockey teams. They were bonded at a depth of trust that put no subject out of bounds.

"Perseus never knew for sure who his real dad was and at least I got to meet mine."

"And now this dad you love so much is moving away, Minka," Andrea said, her voice quieting. Before Minka could respond, Andrea went on, "And since I won the bet I get to ask you some questions." She opened Minka's mythology book to the page with Aunt Nina Judd's handwriting and asked Minka to read it.

Minka began reading out loud:

"Dear, Dear Ellie! If you're now looking at this book of children's myths I read to your Kate and Jamie growing up, something very special has happened. You are a grandmother! That means either Jamie kept her precious baby girl or Kate's now a mother or, Dear God willing, both."

Minka let out a belly laugh. "It sounds just like the Aunt Nina I've heard stories about my whole life. I wish I'd known her."

Then Minka grew serious. "And, yes, I'm the baby Mom 'kept.' But, Andrea, I have to be honest—as if I could be anything else with you—that word has bothered me since I saw this note in the myth book. And I'm too afraid to ask my mom because the only meaning I can think of is…well, just not one I want to think about."

Andrea took a deep breath and said, "Give you up for adoption?"

Minka just stared. After a pause she asked gently, "How come you know my mind almost before I do, Andrea?"

"Oh, Minka, our souls have overlapped since the day I was the Pied Piper playing the flute that attracted your goofy Pogo. And, no, I wouldn't want to have explored the word 'kept' either for the same reason you haven't!

"But let's just say your fears are right. Think about it, Minka. Your mom is a single woman with an unplanned pregnancy—that has to be a given, right?"

Minka hesitated, then nodded.

"Add to that because she wanted to come home to take care of her Aunt Nina dying from cancer, your mom cut short her treatment for alcoholism in Arizona. So that puts her at high risk for relapsing when she's watching her beloved Aunt Nina get sicker every day. Plus she has no money and no home!"

"Mom had the log cabin," Minka said wanting to shut down every excuse behind 'kept.'

21

"Oh, no she didn't. You told me Aunt Nina left the cabin to your mother in her will, and Aunt Nina didn't die until the next spring, Minka."

Pogo recognized the stress in the room, and lumbered over to push his head under Minka's hand where she began scratching his grey-tipped black ears as she spoke. "I know what you're trying to tell me, Andrea. My mother had so many good reasons for giving me away, but she didn't. So I should be grateful to her."

Andrea started to laugh until her coughing interrupted her. When she could talk again, she said in her teasing voice, "Now who's the mind reader, Minka!"

"My turn to be winner winner chicken dinner," Minka said and started to giggle. Andrea was still catching her breath when Andrea's grandmother opened the door.

"You two are always laughing about something funny." Nana said. "But now it's lunch time," she turned around just in time to miss the eye rolls Andrea and Minka exchanged.

"Ten minutes please," Andrea called after her.

"No longer! You need to eat, my dear!" Nana said closing the door.

Andrea turned to Minka. "Okay. Now we've settled the 'kept' question, I need you to explain the other part of Aunt Nina's note."

"Where she says my grandmother Ellie would have opened a children's recipe book, but never one on Greek myths?"

"That's what I don't get," Andrea asked.

Minka smiled as she rubbed Pogo's ears. "Aunt Nina was dying when she wrote this note for my grandmother Ellie Cameron who was a cateress and Aunt Nina's best friend."

"Wow," Andrea said with a huge smile. "What a funny and wise woman your namesake was! Sort of like the Oracle at Delphi foreseeing the future. That Kate would get to be a mother."

"I never thought of it that way, Andrea. But you're right. So does that mean Aunt Nina knows about the twins? I'd like to think so. But I'm just not sure about the afterlife."

Andrea folded her hands in a sort of prayerful gesture. "Nobody is sure, my new best friend. But after I saw my chart, I ordered a book about near death experiences with glimpses into the afterlife. Obviously," she said touching the small gold cross on her neck. "I want very much to believe there is."

"Hey! We're not talking about that, remember?" Minka said forcefully.

"Right. But speaking about the afterlife makes me think of being born and what I keep forgetting to ask you. What day in November were you born?"

"November 7."

At that Andrea yelled with all the breath she had. "I knew it! I knew it. We're both Scorpios! My birthday is October 30! I should have figured this out sooner."

"As in scorpion? So we're both spiders?" Minka started laughing.

"Don't laugh. This is serious. You know what Scorpios are best known for?"

"I've never paid much attention to the Zodiac."

"You should because, get this, Scorpios are known for their capacity to have deep friendships. And loyalty. Does that sound like anyone you know?"

Minka was quiet a moment. "Andrea, the day I met you I had this gut feeling I already knew you. Like we'd been friends before." She watched a patch of sunlight cross the floor. "Maybe there is something to the Zodiac, because how we even know each other is like, well, destiny."

"Our Scorpio stars were aligned," Andrea said. "And you know why else I believe it? Another strong trait Scorpios have is intense determination. And who's more determined than you to keep both your mom and dad and who's more determined than I am to breathe..." A hand bell ring from the dining room cut Andrea off.

"Coming," Andrea said easing into her wheelchair. As Minka and Pogo followed her, Andrea said quietly over her shoulder, "And I have another major secret to tell you."

{ 5 }

Promises To Keep

SATURDAY NOVEMBER 20, 2020

As she turned into the Sandpiper driveway, Jamie quickly blew into her palm to see if her breath stunk of garlic. It was an unpleasant side affect of Antabuse, and she could smell it now. She wished it didn't. But, actually, she didn't really care if the pill had stopping her from drinking today.

She was surprised to see Casey's unmarked police sedan with the roof light parked in front of the Sandpiper. The first thing he'd done after marrying Ellie seven years before was apply for a permit to build a garage behind the cottage. He had to be able to get on the road any time day and night even in Michigan blizzards.

But between the U.S. Army Corps of Engineers' and Spring Port Township's regulations, building anywhere near Lake Michigan was a challenge—even for Spring Port's Chief of Police. After months of wrangling, Casey got a permit to build a minimally sized two-car garage, but so far back from the Sandpiper, it was a cold trek in the winter.

Since it was Saturday, Jamie assumed he'd been on a call and left his car out. She parked her Subaru behind his car and saw Maddie pull in behind her. Before Jamie could close her car door, Maddie had her in a powerful bear hug. Petite as Maddie was, her years of heavy housework doing her mother's cleaning jobs had given Maddie the muscular development of a fitness trainer.

"I love you, Jamie," Maddie said in her ear. "You gave me a life I never would have had without you. I will always have your back." Jamie bit her lip, hugging Maddie back. "No, no, Jamie. Don't cry," Maddie said feeling the wet cheeks. "You and Minka and everyone in there," she pointed at the Sandpiper, "are my family too. Whatever this is about, we'll get through it together."

Jamie kissed Maddie's freckled cheek. "As we will deal with Ben's problems. Together."

"So are you guys coming in or just hanging out in the driveway?" Ellie called from the open door. "Pete and Kate are dropping the twins off at their babysitters–oh, but there they are just pulling in by the cabin.

"Maddie, I'm so glad to see you," Ellie said grabbing Maddie in a bear hug. "I ran into your cute friend Ben at Meijer's not long ago." Maddie looked over her shoulder at Jamie who raised her eyebrows knowingly.

"Hey, Jamie," Kate said grabbing her younger sister's hand, "blood oath remember?"

"Forever and always," Jamie said squeezing Kate's hand.

As the four of them moved inside, the sweet scent of baked goods filled the air. "Please tell me those are your goodie bars I'm smelling, Ellie," Pete said.

They all knew Ellie's first reaction for dealing with trouble was to make food. Bars and cookies were her favorite remedies. "You're my best customer, Pete," Ellie said handing him a goodie bar in a napkin. "My girls worry about the calories, but I'm glad you don't. You're as lean as the day you and Kate got married so my sweets haven't hurt you a bit."

"She never says that to me," Casey Brennan said putting his big arm around Ellie's shoulders. "I've stopped weighing myself since I got this beauty to marry me," he kissed the top of her head.

Jamie gave Casey a pat on the back. Her mother truly was a beauty. Almost 60, Ellie had a single streak of white in her dark hair that made her almost more striking. Her olive skin was smooth, with only some laugh lines around her eyes. Ellie Cameron Brennan still turned heads–and her besotted husband Casey knew it.

"Same rules as always," Ellie said, "on the drinks. Help yourselves to what you want to. Fresh coffee, ice tea, Diet Coke."

Out of respect for Jamie's sobriety, the family never drank alcohol around her. Jamie hadn't asked them not to, but she was grateful for the show of support. She also knew it meant they understood how challenging her recovery was. Never more than right now.

Holding the warm goodie bar up, Pete said to Kate as he sat down beside her, "Here's why I married you, sweetheart!"

Kate rolled her eyes. "Proves how smart you are because your wife still doesn't like to cook," she said passing the plate of bars to Jamie next to her.

Picking one up, Jamie said, "Remember we recovering alcoholics need our sugar to replace the booze. Thank you all for coming on such short notice. After we talk, I'm going to meet Gloria at the Club for a meeting. I need one. This won't take long."

With a deep inhale, Jamie began. "One of many things we Cameron women learned from Aunt Nina was to speak up if we had something to say. Especially when it's hard stuff." As she felt Kate reach under the table with a supporting pat on her leg, Jamie swallowed against her racing heart.

"Keith called me this morning to say he wants to meet with me alone next week to talk about," her voice broke, "about custody."

"Custody! That's bullshit!" Pete, who rarely cursed, exclaimed amidst the other gasps around the table. "He's the scoundrel who violated every canon of medical ethics by having an affair with you when he was your psychiatrist…."

"No, no, Pete," Jamie cut him off. "You all need to know this. I was the one who took advantage of him. It's been part of my sickness. Teasing men to make me feel better about myself." The headline flashed across her eyes. 'Local Pilot Dies in Bridge Accident.' But it wasn't an accident. Her boss Roger Hamper had driven his car off the Spring Port bridge.

After a pause, Jamie continued. "Yes, Pete, you're right that Keith isn't the good guy we all thought he was. But I can't blame what happened at Saguaro on him. And no matter what, we have Minka."

"I give you that, Jamie," Kate said putting an arm around her younger sister's shoulders. "But remember when Mom and Casey got married and we all thought Keith was going to buy Casey's house and move here to be near Minka? And now he's trying to take her away from you? From us?" she opened her palms toward everyone.

"No, I'm sorry Jamie," Kate said, shaking her head. "This is all on him! Tearing our Minka's life apart!"

"Oh, my dear Jamie," Ellie's voice broke as she reached across the table to grab her daughter's hands. "We won't let him have her!!"

"Does Minka know?" Maddie asked leaning toward Jamie for an answer.

"Not yet," Jamie said. "I've talked to her about how sorry I am she won't have weekends with her dad anymore. But Minka never says anything. I think it makes her too sad."

"That's what worries me most," Maddie said. "You know Minka's my little sister who tells me everything. But she's avoided any conversation about her dad's moving."

"Same here," Ellie said. "I brought it up one day last summer when Minka and I were on a beach walk and her response was to jump in the lake and swim out to the sandbar."

"All right, people," Casey's commanding voice took over as he raised his big hand to quiet them. "Let's get down to business here. We need to hear Jamie out before we get all stirred up about anything."

Jamie nodded at him, grateful for the chance to get it all out before she broke down.

She took a deep yoga breath, and began. "Keith called first thing this morning to say he'd like to take Minka out for a late Thanksgiving lunch next week. He asked me first to make sure it was okay, which he's always done and I've appreciated. And I know he wants as much time with Minka as he can get since he's moving right after Christmas. But then he said he wanted to talk to me alone after lunch when he brought Minka home."

"I'm sure you asked him why," Maddie said her dark eyes staring hard at Jamie.

"I did," Jamie nodded slowly. "Twice, because he sounded funny, even evasive." Then she looked around at everyone before she went on. "When he finally answered, I only heard that one word. And I was so knocked out by it I don't think I even spoke again. He just said he'd see us next Friday and hung up."

The rumbling sound of the November wind blowing off Lake Michigan filled the room. Finally Casey broke the shocked silence. "We can't jump to conclusions, people. For all we know Keith might just want to make plans about arranging visiting times with Minka next summer. Or spring break. I think he's just making sure he can still see Minka after he moves to Tucson."

"Casey's right," Ellie said. "Divorced parents always make custody arrangements so children have time with both of them. I mean this is not a divorce, but it's still the same because they have a child together."

Jamie looked out at the low grey clouds over the Big Lake wanting with all her heart to believe them. But there had been a tension in Keith's voice this morning she'd never heard before. "Thank you both for that optimism, Casey and Mom. But I have to prepare for what I'm so afraid he means. We've all heard him say Minka's the most important thing in his life. What if he's going to ask for custody so she can move with him?"

"But that could never happen!" Pete said firmly. "You're the mother. He can't take her away."

"He's her father and custody can go to the parent who's best for the child,"

Jamie said quietly.

"Well, nonsense, Jamie." Ellie said. "No one's a better mother than you."

"But it's about who is the better parent, Mom. A single mother who's a newly recovering alcoholic with a history of relapses or a respected married psychiatrist with a bestselling book on recovery?"

Now Jamie could hold back her tears no longer, wiping her cheeks with a napkin as Kate pulled her sister into her arms.

"Casey," Pete asked. "You work in law enforcement so you know how the system works. Mothers always get custody over dads, don't they? You know the courts better than we do."

Everybody looked at Casey, but Jamie. The problem was the town's top law officer knew too much about how judges decide custody disputes. The father, Dr. Summers with a successful, financially stable career now married to Pat who loves Minka–or Jamie, an unwed alcoholic mother.

Spring Port's Chief of Police sat motionless as his silence filled the room.

{ 6 }

Promises To Keep

SATURDAY NOVEMBER 20
5:30 AA MEETING

Wrapped in a purple down coat, Jamie's AA sponsor Gloria Cook was waiting just outside the flat-roofed brown brick building in the middle of a huge parking lot filled with cars. Two blocks from Lake Michigan, the Harbor Alano Club had recently moved from its original converted house on Third Street into this former office building.

The new location didn't have the hominess of the lilac-bushed old Victorian house. But it did have the dozen rooms needed for the different support groups to hold their separate meetings. While more and more people continued to come to Alcoholics Anonymous meetings, the major reason for the jump in attendance the past year was the growing number of people, many of them young, addicted to opioids and heroin.

The slanted light from a late Indian summer sun sparkled on Gloria's ebony hair making her huge smile shine even brighter on her perfect white teeth. Gloria had an iron fist when Jamie needed it. But she also had an endless supply of unconditional love for her challenging sponsee.

"Hey, girlfriend," Gloria grabbed Jamie's hand between two of her own. A deacon in her church, Gloria had 16 years of recovery. And while Jamie's relapses devastated Gloria, she lived by the four letters on her green wristband. *What Would Jesus Do.* He'd forgive "seventy times seven times," she told Jamie.

"I knew when you called to meet me, something bad is goin' on, Jamie. We got a few minutes before the meeting. Let's go find a quiet place inside before we blow away in this wind."

They walked into the club's small lobby, a big framed poster of the 12 Steps on the wall, and headed down the hallway until they saw through one door's window that no one was in there. Jamie closed the door behind them as Gloria pulled two small water bottles out of her big red purse, handing one to Jamie. As they sat down on grey stackable chairs, Gloria said, "I'm real afraid I know what this about, Jamie. And just prayin' hard I'm wrong."

Jamie uncapped the water bottle, and drank half in one swig before answering. "Keith wants to talk to me about custody the day after Thanksgiving, Gloria." Jamie's face flushed as she said it.

"Dear God in Heaven," Gloria leaned back as if raising her face to Him and shook her head. "If I was still a cussin' woman I'd peel off some good ones right now." Then she looked hard at Jamie. "This is no excuse to start drinking, Jamie. Do you hear me, Girl? None!"

"I knew you'd say that, Gloria. Yes, drinking was my first reaction. And, well, you know I can't stay sober if I'm not vigorously honest. I'm sorry, but I took an Antabuse this morning."

Gloria took Jamie's hands in hers. "Girlfriend, I smelled it on you right away, but I needed you to tell me yourself. Of course I wish you hadn't. You know I'm by-the-book AA and don't cotton to that stuff. But you did tell me the truth. And I can see you've been rocked by his talkin' custody.

"And I have to tell you it's rockin' me too right now, Jamie, cuz here I'm the one who helped find Minka's dad! Lied to you to do it!" she shook her head. "This happenin' because I lied and Joe lied and you trusted us and now you're being punished all because of us!"

"No, no, Gloria. I just went through this with Mother and everyone. Minka knows her dad. She's had seven years with him. He'll be in her life always and no one wants to take that away...."

Jamie chugged the rest of her water. "I don't know what he means by 'custody,' but I'm scared to death, Gloria. What if he wants to take her away—away from me?" Jamie's voice broke.

"Did that man never hear about King Solomon and the baby?"

The door opened, and a voice called in, "Time for the meeting ladies."

"Thanks," Gloria said back. "Jamie, this is where you need to be right now," she pointed at the floor. "This is where you need to talk about it."

As they left the room, a tall man in a business suit walked by them. "Hi, Paul," Gloria greeted him. "Good to see you again. It's been a while."

"Gloria. Jamie. I need to be here," he said in a subdued voice.

"That makes two of us," Jamie replied.

As they followed Paul, Gloria whispered, "This feels bad" so quietly Jamie barely heard her and continued to murmur inaudible words. Then Jamie realized what she couldn't really hear. Gloria was praying.

They followed Paul into Room B, the No First Drink meeting Jamie and Gloria went to this time of day. People were just starting to gather around a long metal table as Gloria sat down next to Paul, Jamie beside her. The usual chatter of friends greeting each other seemed to quiet down as they saw Paul.

When everyone was seated, a round-faced woman with short-cut white hair said in a Boston-accented voice, "Good afternoon. I'm Carrie, a grateful alcoholic. I'm chairing today and I welcome everyone to the 5:30 No First Drink meeting of the Harbor Alano Club of Alcoholics Anonymous. Will you please join me in the Serenity Prayer.

With bowed heads, the group spoke in unison, "*God grant me the serenity to accept the things I cannot change, the courage to change the things I can,* the group recited together, *and the wisdom to know the difference.*"

"Now," Carrie said half looking at Paul, "does anyone have a topic they'd like to talk about today?"

With a clear strain in his voice and signaling with one hand, Paul said, "Yes. I do, Carrie." Now his voice cracked. "Grief. And if I can, I'd like to start."

"Please do, Paul," Carrie said gently.

"Hello, my name's Paul, and I am a grateful recovering alcoholic."

"Hi, Paul," the room responded.

"Most of you have heard me talk about my niece," he paused, "my beautiful Jennifer, the girl I helped raise when her alcoholic father abandoned the family. And we all know it's a family disease." Around the room, people nodded their acknowledgement of this hard reality.

"Jenn began smoking pot in high school, then went to college and began binge drinking like so many freshmen do.

"But, unfortunately for Jenn, she was her dad's daughter and my niece. She inherited the gene from both sides of the family. In college, alcohol took over her life as it had mine around the same age. But my miraculous luck was that I had a roommate whose uncle was in recovery. The uncle took me to my first AA meeting and got me into the program. I've been sober for almost 25 years."

"Hear, hear," someone called out. Paul raised his hand in thanks for the praise.

"But while it was obvious to me what was happening with Jenn, my sister Rachel, Jenn's mom, seldom drinks so she couldn't see what I did. Grades dropping. Missing classes. I even drove to Jenn's dorm in Kalamazoo last year and offered to pay if she'd go into rehab—even though I knew what everyone here knows she'd say.

"Never mind that her room was a pit and her face was puffy and her clothes disheveled, Jenn gave me that million dollar smile and said, 'Hey, Uncle Paul, 'I'm cool. Everyone parties here. I've got it under control.' Her breath reeked of booze. But I still mailed her a brochure from the Brighton Recovery hospital knowing she'd deep six it.

"What I didn't know was that it wasn't just alcohol anymore. Somehow she'd also gotten hooked on the painkiller OxyContin." He paused looking down at his hands.

"This is where it hits too close to home. Many of you know I'm an ER doctor so I treat trauma patients. In the mid-1990s, this new miracle pain-killer OxyContin came along at the same time the medical journals started reporting that we physicians weren't treating pain like we should. Thank you," he said to Carrie who'd brought him a bottle of water.

Shaking his head, Paul said, "I will have to live with the guilt that I bought into it like almost every other doctor at the time. OxyContin was like the new Penicillin to make our patients' lives better. We were given all these free samples to start our patients on and then we were encouraged to write refill prescriptions for 90 pills at a time." He twisted the bottle cap off and took a big drink.

"So, yes, we doctors carry the burden of over prescribing the painkiller. But at the time we had no idea how much money the drug company was spending to promote this miracle painkiller as safe and non-addictive. A brand-new drug made by a respectable pharmaceutical company? And all my trauma patients had legitimate pain? Why wouldn't we prescribe this new drug for them? Why would we question that?"

Paul took another swig, the room so silent his swallowing could be heard. "You know," Paul looked around the room, "what happened next. Purdue is now being sued by the government and more people are dying every day from an opioid overdose. And will continue to.

"And, no. I didn't forget my topic. And I think maybe you realized I needed this extra time to give me the courage to tell what I came to say."

Gloria laid her fleshy hand on Paul's shoulder as he began. "Last summer

Jenn got arrested for the third time shoplifting to buy heroin, the cheap version of Oxycontin. Jenn went to jail for seven months. Many of you will understand why Rachel and I were both grateful she got caught." Several people around the table nodded.

"She'd be safe locked up. And we hoped in jail she'd be off heroin long enough for her head to clear and to think about going into rehab. While she was still in jail, Jenn told her mother she'd never been through such physical hell as she did withdrawing on the cold cement floor of her cell. Rachel asked me why Jenn would *ever* use again after that?

"But Rachel isn't in the program so she doesn't get it. There's a reason the Big Book calls it a 'disease of insanity.' So, three weeks ago Jenn was released and went home with Rachel. 'Never going to use again,' she swore and promised. Then the two of them spent a week doing mother-daughter things together—shopping, manicures, all the fun stuff.

"Then the first Saturday after jail, Jenn said she was meeting Helen, her best friend growing up." Paul hunched his shoulders. "What Jenn didn't know was that one relapse could kill her immediately. I didn't warn her because, well, I wanted too much to believe with Rachel that Jennifer was done."

Gloria pulled tissues out of a Kleenex box on the table and handed them to Paul. "But after seven months in jail, Jenn's brain had lost the tolerance to morphine she'd built up over her several years of using. One hit could shut down her respiratory system." Paul dabbed his eyes.

"The police found her body at 4 a.m. Sunday morning in a car parked by Lighthouse Pier with the hypodermic needle still in her arm." The air filled with gasps as some covered their mouths in horror that pretty, young Jenn's life could end like that.

"Jenn had never talked to Helen," Paul said quietly.

Jamie knew the shocked reaction to that was not from surprise. Paul had named the topic. But, still, hearing the actual words, visualizing this beautiful young woman dead on the seat of a car with a hypodermic needle sticking out of her arm, the ending still stunned them. Gloria pulled Paul toward her like a mother comforting a child, her own dark skin shining with tears.

His voice thick, Paul said, "One last thing I need to share. You know, because of my work, I do all I can to promote organ transplants. All my family members have the red heart next to 'Donor' on their driver's licenses. Jennifer did too. But," he stopped to drink the water, "she'd been dead too long for her major organs to be harvested. What I want you to know is that maybe the only comfort to Rachel and me is that Jenn's young healthy bones, corneas, and skin could be transplanted and are now making life better for several other people."

Out of the mournful silence, a big man wearing a Redwings cap began quietly clapping. Soon, tears still rolling down some of their faces, everyone in the room joined him.

"Hi," Gloria said after the room quieted down, "my name is Gloria, and I'm a grateful recovering alcoholic. And if you don't already have that heart on your license, get yourselves to the Secretary of State tomorrow. You all know there's just three outcomes for us alcoholics and addicts. The first two are recovery or jail. Tomorrow," Gloria's boss voice echoed. "And with that I'll pass."

Jamie was next. "Hi. I'm Jamie, a grateful recovering alcoholic."

"Hi, Jamie," the group responded.

"I planned to pass–even though Gloria thought it would help me to share today. But now, hearing Paul, I can't pass. And I know we don't like cross talk, but I just have to tell you directly, Paul," Jamie looked at him, "you have to forgive yourself. How could you have guessed a company whose drugs you'd always used was now lying to doctors about a new one? And even though alcohol is my drug of choice, not heroin, I can be so in Jennifer's head that first night she got free!

"I'm out of jail and my lie about Helen worked. There is no way in he…" Jamie looked toward Gloria, "no way in the world that any warning from Uncle Paul about lowered tolerance would have stopped me anymore than it could have stopped Jennifer."

Paul looked over at Jamie, and said softly, "Thank you."

Jamie gave Paul the peace sign. "But I owe you, Paul. I came here today looking for support for me. My daughter Minka's father is moving to Arizona and suddenly he wants to talk about custody. Everyone here knows what Minka means to me and I can feel your support. Thank you. The only reason I'm not crying is that listening to Paul brought back to me the Prayer of Saint Francis. Some time ago Gloria made me memorize it–and you know I do what Gloria tells me to!"

Even Paul joined the chorus of chuckles, an obvious relief from the heavy discussion.

"I just want to say," Jamie went on, "that I'm grateful to this program for reminding me that whatever we suffer, others have it worse. Paul and Rachel have lost Jenn forever. I can still hope that 'custody' doesn't mean Keith wants to take my daughter to Arizona."

Jamie didn't see Gloria, the devout Baptist, make the Catholic sign of the cross.

"And if the worst happens," she paused as her voice broke, "even then, even then, my Minka would still be alive. Would you pray with me," Jamie said bowing her head.

"Saint Francis called us to: *Not so much seek to be consoled as to console, To be understood as to understand, To be loved as to love.*"

{ 7 }

Promises To Keep

MONDAY NOVEMBER 22, 2010

"Hey, Ben," Gerald Reynolds, a ruddy-faced Meijer's store manager in his mid-50s, called to Ben Hughes who was pushing a dolly full of boxes out of the storeroom. "I need to talk to you. Come on back in the office with me."

Ben felt the familiar blood rush, but from fear, not dope this time. How long had it been since he'd felt fear? He tried to remember through the fog thickening in his head. Then he did. It was last week when the Lowe's security guard almost caught him leaving the store with his backpack full of copper tubing he hadn't paid for. The one-time star running back at Spring Port High couldn't sprint like he used to, but he was still good enough to leave the bellied guard behind in Lowe's parking lot. He shot up the money he got for the copper in two days.

"Sit down, Ben," Mr. Reynolds patted the folding chair's seat as he sat on another one. "You know I like you, Ben. Always have. Know your mom and dad and grandparents too."

Ben knew that's how he got this job as a Meijer floor stocker.

"I went to most of your games and still remember you as a junior running past everyone on the field to score the winning touchdown in the Tri-County Championship."

Ben tried to tamp down his twitches so he could focus on what his boss was saying. He could feel the sweat on his chest added to the body odor he knew he already had.

"My wife and I were also at the game your senior year when you had that horrible leg fracture." He shook his head as he said, "We all thought you took a late hit that didn't get called."

Ben shuddered at the memory, still hearing the crack of bone breaking as it pierced his skin. So long ago. His whole life ago.

"I can see you're nervous, Ben. I think you know why you're here."

"The thing with Adam you mean?" Ben finally heard his own voice speaking through his dry mouth, every muscle in his body aching. He'd been through the hell of withdrawal before. He just had to tough it out until he got some smack. "Just a little go-around between friends." Ben's bowels began to cramp and he knew diarrhea was next.

"Not 'little,' Ben," Mr. Reynolds voice, harsher now, broke in. "Adam chipped a front tooth when you shoved him against a wall. You're lucky he is your friend and doesn't want to press charges or you'd be in jail. Meijer is taking care of the dental bill, but we just can't have this, Ben.

"It's just not like you to bully someone, especially since Adam's so much smaller than you. But I've seen changes in you these past few months. Some of your Meijer team members have talked to me about you too. Coming in late. Looking 'strung out,' is how they put it.

"Just look at yourself right now. Your hair is filthy. You look like you haven't shaved in a month. And I don't need to tell you what you smell like."

Ben dug his long fingernails into the skin on his upper arms just above the needle bruises. Just below the hemp leaf tattoo. Oh, how his parents had freaked out about that! His mother still wouldn't look at him without a shirt on. Ben scratched harder like he could dig the tattoo and the needle marks away. Trying not to smell his own body stink. Trying not to fidget.

Reynolds paused, waiting for Ben to answer. To explain. To defend himself. After the silence, Reynolds put his hands on his knees and said, "We think you're on something, Ben. We're hearing a lot about crystal meth around here lately. And even heroin. Maybe it's just booze. We don't know, but we're worried."

"No, no, no. I'm an athlete," Ben struggled to seem alert but his shaky voice wasn't helping. "You know, you, you know that, Mr. Reynolds.. Not me. No drugs for me." But then his chin suddenly hit his chest. "Ben!" Mr. Reynolds said in shock as he stared at him.

Ben jerked his head up. He had fooled people for so long he didn't know how to answer. When his parents saw the leaf on his shoulder, they yelled at him about smoking pot. He'd told them all his high school friends did, which was true in the beginning. What he didn't say was that he had different friends now. New ones who'd moved on to opioids. And now, heroin.

Since he'd moved into his parents' basement when his roommate kicked him out of their apartment, his mom and dad kept harping about his smoking marijuana. His mom had never noticed when her leftover bottle of Vicodin from foot surgery went missing. They were clueless about the dope.

Only lately Maddie Langston suspected. He knew she was too smart for him. For anyone, really. But he'd had a crush on her since the day he'd beaten up the psycho kid bullying her. She never knew he liked her because he was the big shot senior athlete while Maddie was just a freshman with a sketchy family.

But then last spring they'd run into each other at Walgreen's. She was buying lipstick and he was picking up a prescription for OxyContin. He'd found a new doctor in Muskegon after his own refused to write any more for him.

Maddie was even prettier in her twenties than in high school. As he quickly stuffed the new bottle of pain pills in his jacket pocket, he found out she'd graduated from college and was running the Sandpiper Foundation. He'd heard she inherited some money. But there were always wild rumors in Spring Port.

When he found out she'd just broken up with her boyfriend, he asked her out. They'd started seeing each other. And he found out the rumor was true. Maddie had inherited money from the old Russian lady who was murdered in her antique store. And by the same psycho guy who'd name-called Maddie in high school. Ben knew Maddie had really cared for Aunt Annie, and she never talked about what happened. And Ben never asked.

Recently Maddie had started looking at him differently. Keeping him at a distance. He knew she was suspicious.

"Well, Ben," Gerald Reynolds broke into his thoughts, "you know Meijer takes good care of its employees. Because you've had a good work record for over two years, instead of letting you go, which I was afraid would happen, they've agreed to my suggestion. They're offering to hold your job for 90 days on the condition you get some help. They're continuing your insurance so you can find the resources you need. You just have to document whatever medical treatment you get for the HR people if you want your job back."

Ben struggled to sound normal even though his brain could hardly process what he'd just heard. He'd gotten good at nodding his head as people talked to him so he could appear more cognitive than he was. But this stress about his job had accelerated the craving.

The bite had been taking over sooner and sooner lately. The sucking pain that demanded the dope because nothing else mattered. Not Mr. Reynolds or Meijer or Maddie or his family. Who were they anyway? No. Only the baggie with the tan powder in his jeans pocket mattered.

Mumbling some thank yous and taking the papers Mr. Reynolds handed him, Ben made it out the door before he stumbled. If Mr. Reynolds saw that, Ben didn't care anymore. All he cared about was reaching his car. He almost knocked a woman over running as fast as he could make himself through the employee parking lot, pulling the lifesaving baggie out of his pocket.

Ben fumbled with his car keys, his head exploding with the urgency. He fell into the car and grabbed his kit from under the seat. It held his life, the tools of his survival. Wrapping his seatbelt tightly around his left upper arm as a tourniquet, Ben pulled the plunger out of his hypodermic needle to draw in liquid from his plastic water bottle. Then forcing his hands to be steady, he carefully poured the precious tan powder into a spoon and dripped in water to mix up the heroin.

Snapping on the lighter from his kit to heat the spoon and dissolve the mixture, Ben put a nub of a Cue Tip on top of the dope to filter out any particles. Then he pulled the miracle fluid up from the spoon into his hypodermic needle with the desperation of a drowning man seeking air. "Get this rig in," he called out loud to the now amber liquid, his animal brain screaming as he plunged the needle deep into his swollen arm vein.

Ben lay back on the seat and waited. Waited for the warm blanket, the heavy blanket that sent heat into the marrow of his bones. The pure comfort, the soft light that filled his whole body with the impossible release he craved. The sweep of pleasure that lifted him so high he could touch the moon and stars.

But it didn't happen. And Ben couldn't remember when it had first stopped working. When he'd had to start shooting up more and more to feed the beast gnarling in his head.

How long had it been since the dope stopped delivering the high it once did? How long since the music stopped? He felt the drug unfold into his body, but not with any real happiness. Just the cessation of craving. The demon had been fed. And all it gave back was a sense of Ben being himself, the belly cramps easing. For the moment, Ben felt normal.

And even as the drug slowly relieved his terrifying cravings, Ben knew it wouldn't last long. The truculent dragon in his head would need to be fed again. He had to call Horse. He fumbled for the cell phone in his jacket. He couldn't fall asleep yet. Horse was his man. His dealer. His lifeline….

"This you?" Horse answered on the first ring.

"Hey, Horse. Yah. It's me. I need some hits. Today, man, I can't wait. Can you get me like ten of the two grams?"

"Benny, Benny, Benny Boy," Horse said in his smoke scratched voice. "You know you already into my shit for the last two deliveries. I ain't your bank, Ben. No dope until you pay what you owe. And cold cash from now on. Credit days are over."

"Hey, Horse. You can't do that," Ben felt a sense of panic. "I am good for the money. You know that. How long we been doing business, and I ain't stiffed you ever."

"So how come you owe me for the last two times? Huh? Sorry. It's cash and carry for you from now on, my friend. Get somebody else to front you. I'm done."

"Horse. I just lost my job," Ben wished he didn't hear the whine in his voice.

Horse actually laughed until his smoker's cough stopped him.

"Now there's a serious news flash! A junkie losing a job. So get into your old man's wallet. Oh, wait. Didn't I hear that old lady who got offed left your new chick a major chunk of coin? Get it from her."

"I can't ask her for money. She's already on to me I think."

"Hey, Dude. Did you hear me say 'ask'? 'Get' means 'get.' Do what you gotta do to the bitch! But you better get me the cash, Benjamin," any early cordiality now dripped with menace. "Don't think you want the Cuchillo to come calling. You live with Mommy and Daddy, don't you?" The phone clicked off.

Ben felt a frisson of fear that even the dope couldn't make up for. The Mexican named for his instrument of choice was the known muscle in the lakeshore drug world. Just hearing his name was enough. Ben's chest tightened in desperation. His dad never left his billfold out and his mother kept her purse with her. And even when they were home they kept their bedroom door locked. Maybe he hadn't fooled his parents after all.

But Maddie. Sweet, trusting Maddie. After he found out the rumor about her inheritance was true, he still never asked about it because it didn't matter to him. Ben cared about Maddie, not her money. He wished he didn't know what happened to his friend Eddie's finger after he'd stiffed his dealer.

Horse's words echoed in his head. "Do what you gotta do."

{ 8 }

Promises To Keep

FRIDAY AUGUST 20, 2010

Minka was glad to see Pogo bound toward the stairs leading to the front deck of the Armitage's cottage. She thought it meant Andrea felt good enough to sit outside where she could see the lake. She hoped so, anyway. Hard as Minka tried not to see it, she couldn't miss Andrea's working harder to breathe over recent weeks. Maybe she was better today, Minka told herself.

Minka skipped up the steps to hear Andrea's happy voice saying, "Hey, you, Rascal Dog." Then as Minka rounded the corner of the cottage, the coughing began. Pogo's head was again in Andrea's lap where she sat in a padded lounge chair.

"No wheelchair!" Minka said in an upbeat tone. "And you're right where you always want to be looking at the lake. So the wind didn't force you indoors today!" Minka kissed Andrea's pale cheek, hugging her as hard as she dared. "Are the black flies bothering you?"

"How would you know that, my young friend?"

"Who grew up on this side of the lake and who lived on the wrong side of it?"

"Chicago is not the wrong side, Miss Know it All. We get to see the sun rise and you only get to see it go down."

"And who has not missed a sunset since you came here this summer?" Minka said back.

"Look who's got all the answers today," Andrea said as Minka sat down in the canvas chair beside the lounge. "Another Winner Winner for you, Minka. But you are right, my sweet young friend. I really will miss the sunsets when we have to leave this 'Big Lake' as you call it."

Minka felt her sadness start to rise. And, as she always could, Andrea recognized it. "But we're not talking about that because you haven't answered me yet about the flies. See this?" she held up a yellow-screened fly swatter. "I've killed at least five already."

"I don't see any bodies?" Minka looked at the floor around Andrea.

"Think you got me, don't you. But you know my mother's a worry wart so she's been sweeping them up faster than I can kill them. She's not going to have any dirty stuff around me! I'll test her the next time she hears me swat. You'll see."

Minka thought about the sweetness and the unhappiness. Andrea's mother not wanting to believe Andrea had an incurable disease, but then being overly cautious about any potential germs around her daughter. Barbara Armitage knew, but couldn't bear to know, that her daughter's weakened immune system couldn't risk any infection.

"So about the biting flies, Minka?"

Minka wet her pointer finger, held it in the air, and told Andrea to do the same thing.

"Can you tell where the wind's coming from?" Minka asked.

Andrea frowned, straining to feel the wind. "So I'm not a Girl Scout and I've never been camping. But," Andrea pointed over her shoulder, "it feels like from behind me."

"Chicken dinner again, Andrea. And what direction is that?"

"I'm looking west toward Chicago so the opposite direction means the wind is out of the east."

"You got it. And when the wind comes from the east, it blows the flies out of the trees."

"So you're telling me I can sit out here by the lake today because the house is protecting my breathing from the wind since it's coming from the east? And this same east wind letting me look at the lake is also bringing the stable flies to bite my legs with it?"

"'Stable' flies?" Minka asked. "I never heard that before. They're black flies and they especially love ankles."

"At the barn in Libertyville where I kept my horse, they call them stable flies. They draw blood biting horses just like they do from people."

As if he were listening, Pogo opened his mouth and snapped at a fly buzzing around his head sending both girls into noisy laughter. "You're going to get my mother out here if you're not careful, Big Boy," Andrea said scratching Pogo's head. "But enough about flies! Tell me what's been going on since you were here last time?"

"But I'd like to know why your breathing has sounded worse lately, Andrea?"

Andrea raised both palms in the police 'stop' signal. "I asked first. Then it will be your turn."

"And I want to know all of it, Andrea," Minka looked hard at her friend.

"When have we ever, Minka," Andrea's voice turned deadly serious, "since the first day you pedaled down the driveway, been less than totally honest with each other? That's another quality of Scorpios' deep friendships, if I haven't told you yet."

Minka felt her face flush in embarrassment. "That didn't come out right. It's just that I'm...well, worried. And I have to be honest too!"

"Andrea's mom's been baking again," Nana called as she came out on the deck with a plate of chocolate chip cookies on a tray and two glasses of ice water. "How are you doing on wiping out the stable fly invasion?"

"Yummy, Nana, these are still warm," Andrea said taking a cookie. "And Minka says around here they call them black flies."

"Devil flies, I'd call them," Andrea's grandmother said scanning the deck for dead ones.

"I think Pogo ate one, Nana, so that's one corpse you can tell Mom she doesn't have to sweep up."

"Is she uppity like that with you too, Minka?" Nana asked as she put the glasses on the small table between the girls.

"She tries to be, Nana. But I give it right back."

"Good for you, Minka! She's lucky to have a friend like you," Nana said carrying the empty tray back into the cottage.

Minka waited until the door closed behind her. "All right, I do need your help with what's going on."

"Babe," Andrea turned so she could look Minka full in the face, "there is not one thing I wouldn't do for you. The sicker I get, no, don't interrupt me, I'll get to that–the more I need your friendship."

Minka grabbed Andrea's hand and squeezed it. "And I feel closer to you, Andrea, than anyone else in my life right now." The sound of a powerboat gunning its engine filled the air.

"Here's my problem, Andrea. As much as I keep eavesdropping at the Sandpiper, I never hear anyone talk about my dad's moving to Tucson. So they really don't think it's any big deal."

"That's only because they have no idea how much he's working on you to go with him."

Minka nodded. "And I don't want to tell my mom about it because I'd feel like I'm being disloyal to my dad. Mom would really get upset and call him about it right away. I know she would."

"So you're caught between the people you love the most. And you're betraying your dad if you tell your mom what he's doing and betraying your mom by not telling her."

Minka bobbed her head vigorously. "How do you always understand and say out loud what's in my head but I can't say. Yes! I lose whatever I do."

"Remember Odysseus having to sail between rocks that would destroy his ship and a whirlpool that would sink it?"

"Yes, but not the weird names," Minka said.

"Scylla was the whirlpool and Charybdis the rocks. Now people use the expression 'between a rock and a hard place,'" Andrea said as she took a big drink of water. "That's where you are, my dear Minka. And it's your mom and dad putting you there!" Andrea shook her head, "That is just not fair."

Minka's immediate reaction was to tell Andrea she wasn't one to talk about life's not being fair. But this wasn't the time. Instead she asked, "What should I do?"

Andrea sat silently, looking out at the water as she chewed on her lower lip. Finally, she looked at Minka. "Your dad's not leaving until late December, my dear friend. So what about just going on doing what you are now?

"If you tell your mother about all these little comments he's making about living in Arizona, they'd probably–no for sure they'd have a fight about it. Then for the next, how many months, three? Four? You'll really be in the middle with both your parents. Your mom would start telling you why you have to stay with her, while you're dad would keep pushing Tucson and telling you how much he loves you. That would turn your time at home with your mom into a nightmare, Minka, and ruin the weekends with your dad.

"Makes me think of Procrustes stretching people's bodies to fit his bed. Or cutting their feet off if they were too long. Remember him, Minka?"

"I wish I didn't. I'm already feeling like that and it hasn't started yet. So you're saying if I just keep on being quiet about what my dad says for now, you don't think I'm being disloyal to my mom?"

"No, I don't. Why would she need to know, Minka? She's totally nice about your spending time with your dad now. And she wouldn't be if she knew he was what I have to call bribing you so you'll want to move to Tucson with him."

"Do you really think that's okay, Andrea? You're the person I trust the most. I can't even say how relieved I'd be if you say it's okay for me not to tell my mom."

"Since it's not broken, let's not worry about fixing it. For now anyway. And, my sweet, everybody doesn't need to know everything. That is not being dishonest or disloyal. It's just buying some time."

Minka put her palms together in a prayer and bowed her head toward Andrea like kowtowing in gratitude. "Bless you my wisest, older, dearest friend." Then she sat up and looked into Andrea's gentle eyes. "Now you need to tell me everything, Andrea."

"And I would never do less. And since your family still thinks I'm a Spring Port school friend you and Pogo have been visiting all summer, my news is just for you.

"And I want to tell you, Minka, my family," Andrea nodded her head toward the cottage, "is so glad you spend time with me and they like you so much, they haven't asked questions since the first day. I just told them you had family problems you didn't want to talk about and they respect that. No more questions about Minka Cameron.

"But at some point, our families *will* meet because this friendship," she tapped her heart, "is never going away!" As if he'd heard a change in Andrea's tone, Pogo sat straight up and looked at her. Minka's heart skipped. She'd heard it too.

"You're right that my breathing is worse. Yes, I am getting sicker, my kind young friend. But there is hope. And I need you to help me keep it, Minka."

"Of course! Whatever that hope is, I want it as much as you do, Andrea!"

"I have an appointment at the University of Michigan Hospital, Minka. I'm going to be evaluated for a double lung transplant."

{ 9 }

P r o m i s e s   T o   K e e p

TUESDAY NOVEMBER 23, 2010

The Sandpiper Foundation, started by Nina Judd's investment club and named for the cottage where the women met, was originlly located at the Lakeshore News. Kate had been the first Foundation CEO and because she was also the paper's star columnist, she had free office space there.

The Foundation had been set up when Nina Judd died. Because she was the only one in the investment club who knew—or really cared—about buying stocks, her friends sold the club's assets and created The Sandpiper Foundation.

Knowing how smart Kate was, the women unanimously voted to hire her as the foundation's CEO. But when Kate's long awaited pregnancy produced twins, she immediately gave up her popular newspaper column. She then hired Maddie to take her place at the Foundation. Kate had worked too hard to have children not to be a full-time mother to Sarah and Matt.

Maddie had already donated significant funds to the Sandpiper Foundation from the unexpected inheritance Aunt Annie had left her. The fortune no one knew the antiques dealer had was left to Maddie, the teenager who cleaned her store and the one person who had been kind to Anushka.

Scholarships for talented Spring Port High students would always be the priority mission. Maddie was making sure the Sandpiper Foundation continued the scholarships Aunt Nina and her friends in the investment club had wanted. But now with the significant funds Maddie had donated, the Foundation's assets had opened the door to other good local causes. When Kate left the newspaper and hired Maddie to take her place, the Sandpiper Foundation had moved into a small, but attractive plant-filled office right off main street.

47

"So you see what I see," Maddie said to Gail Ryan, the Foundation's grants officer, as she tapped the papers spread out on the round table in the lobby where they sat. The two offices in back were dark as both women preferred the light from the big front window where they could watch people walking by.

Gail, a petite woman with a spikey haircut, had been a classmate of Maddie's in Grand Valley State's graduate program in Philanthropy and Non-profit Leadership. Now in her late 30s with two children in grade school, despite the age difference, Gail and Maddie had clicked the first time they sat next to each other in class.

"Hello!" Gail exclaimed. "I mean what's not to like about this grant request, Maddie! This Next Step program takes men with non-violent felonies right from prison and trains them in professional construction trades and then finds them jobs? This Jonathan man who started it has beaten the bushes to find companies who will hire these men despite criminal records because they're well trained, highly motivated, and these business owners need their skills. It's a win-win."

"Amen, Sister," Maddie said. "I knew you'd say that. And this request for $50,000 to find counseling and pastoral care for these men during their transitions from prison to the outside world makes perfect sense."

"You think our board will like it as much?" Gail asked.

"You know four of our six board members are children of the women in Nina Judd's original Sandpiper Investment Club. They will always support the scholarships their mothers started. But now with this new money–Maddie never acknowledged it was *her* money–they get just as excited about the other good causes we can now help."

Gail just smiled as she was used to Maddie's talking about the Foundation's 'new' money as if it had dropped from heaven rather than take any credit for her own generosity. The one time Gail had brought up the subject, Maddie cut her off. "Aunt Annie earned every penny of that money working harder and smarter while people around here treated her like dirt. I can take no credit for it."

Gail never mentioned it again. "So about those ladies in the original Sand-piper Club, Maddie, do you know they are still legendary among investment clubs around Michigan for buying Walmart when it went public in 1970? And the only reason they bought it was because it's the same year they started their investment club so they could share birthdays with Walmart."

"I do remember that, Gail," Maddie laughed. "Selling all that Walmart after how many years of stock splits? That was the major contribution to this foundation. That and the young computer company they invested in because smart Kate had one and the ladies liked the name because Michigan has so many apple trees."

Gail shook her head. "No. You can't make that stuff up...." The sound of the front door opening interrupted her.

"Hello, can we help you?" Gail facing the door asked the tall, dark-haired man walking in the door.

"Hey, Ben," Maddie said turning around. "Whoa! Look at you! You sure clean up well," she said with warmth. "I like your short hair! And I'd almost forgotten what you look like without all the facial hair," she rubbed her cheeks, "you had." Maddie felt an unexpected tingle as she saw the handsome man she'd fallen for in high school.

Especially the deep dimple she could again see in Ben's right cheek. To her it marked his sweet nature. Under the tough football player others saw, Maddie had seen a tenderness she adored. When he slammed the psychopathic Albert against lockers for calling Maddie names, she knew it wasn't a show of machismo. It was an act of compassion.

"Hey, Mads. I didn't mean to interrupt you."

"We've just finished up a grant for a non-profit you'd appreciate, Ben. Takes men right from prison and helps them get jobs even with criminal records."

Ben nodded dumbly. Here he was trying to avoid committing a crime and these two women were working on helping criminals.

"This is my friend from high school Ben Hughes, Gail, and this is my partner in crime, Gail Ryan. Oops, bad word choice," Maddie laughed. "My partner in philanthropy."

"Nice to meet you, Gail," Ben reached to shake her hand, trying to ignore the word 'crime.' His smile caught Maddie in the chest.

"Look I can come talk to you later, Maddie. Here or I can drop by your place later."

"Wait just a minute, Ben. We've got how many more grant requests to go through, Gail?" Maddie noticed Gail was staring at Ben in an unusual way.

"What, oh," Gail was caught off guard. "Well, at least a dozen. It's the end of the quarter so everyone sends in at the last minute." She looked at her watch. "It's 1:15. Probably not before five."

Still wondering about the look on Gail's face, Maddie said, "Ben, how about we meet at your favorite Burger King around 5:30 and we can talk there. I'll buy."

For a brief moment, Ben felt relieved. He could put off asking Maddie for money. But then the gut punch of the craving hit him. He couldn't wait that long. "Cool," he strained to sound normal. "See you then," he called over his shoulder as he left. "Nice to meet you..." He couldn't remember her name.

The door hardly closed before Maddie leaned toward her friend. "So what was that beady-eyed look about, Gail?" Maddie asked.

Gail pulled a Kleenex out of her pocket before she answered.

"Do you know Ben well enough to know if he's on something?"

"Like?"

Gail shrugged. "Like drugs? Meth. Pain killers–maybe heroin."

Maddie's stomach churned. "Why–why would you ask such a question?"

"Look, Maddie," Gail laid a hand on Maddie's arm, "the last thing I want to do is upset you. He is dreamy handsome and built like...well, 'buff' people call it. I saw how you looked at him when he walked in. But, Maddie, did you see his eyes? His pupils were big as saucers. And his body movements were too, well, just off. Like tense."

Maddie hadn't noticed the dilated pupils. But she couldn't pretend Ben acted like himself–with his usual casual, easy confidence.

Gail paused to wipe her nose with the Kleenex. "Maddie, remember we gave one of our early grants to Lighthouse Mission in Grand Rapids when it became a men's rehab instead of a homeless shelter?"

"Recovery Strong that's run like a military book camp. You know I remember. Any recovery or mental health grant request goes to the top of my list because of my mother and Jamie."

"Maddie," Gail straightened the papers on the table, "I'm afraid I haven't been as open with you about my family as you have about yours. Almost two years ago, my cousin Jared–he was more like my big brother–got hooked on pain meds after he broke his back falling from a high-lo at work."

"And just like so many people addicted to opioids, Jared moved on to the cheaper heroin when he couldn't afford the expensive prescriptions. Jared ended up overdosing, but he was really lucky because his friend got him to the emergency room before he stopped breathing."

"Oh my dear, Gail," Maddie shook her head sadly. "Jared's story is getting way too familiar these days–except for the part about his getting help in time. The numbers of overdose deaths just keep going up. It's horrifying."

"And, Gail, I'm really glad you told me about Jared. I get why you couldn't before. The shame I felt growing up with my drugged out mother? Only people like us who have loved someone in addiction can understand the awfulness. And I could never stop my mother from drinking and popping pills and nobody could have stopped Jared from using. Where is he now?"

"For my cousin, being so close to dying got his attention. Jared put himself into a rehab in Brighton. Today I'd send him to Recovery Strong, but it wasn't open yet. Jared still lives in a recovery house with other men who've been through rehab. He got his factory job back and has been clean ever since."

"I love that ending, Gail. It recharges my hope for all the rehab programs we support. But, now, well you told me about Jared because of Ben." The two women looked at each other, the unasked question between them.

"Just now Ben reminded me of Jared." Gail played with a pencil on the table. "When he was using, Jared would come ask me for money saying he needed it for rent or he'd get evicted. But I never gave him any because I could see he was coming off a high and trying not to show how desperate he was for a hit. He wasn't going to spend it on rent."

Gail paused, glancing out the window. "Ben's eyes looked like Jared's just now." Gail shook her head. "It was too much deja vu for me, Maddie."

Maddie was hearing what she'd been trying hard not to know when she was with Ben lately. Gail was naming it and Maddie knew she was right. She had learned the signs of addiction as a little girl coming home from school to find her mother on the couch too out of it to make sense talking. By the time she was ten, Maddie had become an expert on signs of substance abuse.

"Ben won't show up tonight, Maddie," Gail broke into her thoughts. "He can't wait that long for his dope."

*   *   *   *

Ben's mouth felt dry as dirt, his heart thumping as he waited in the Meijer parking lot for someone to pull out from a place near the front of the store section where the electronics were located. He'd need to get to his car fast. He'd actually considered the employee lot as he still had his parking pass. But that was farther to run.

Ben hoped he'd made the right decision coming to the same store where he'd worked. He thought if he happened to run into a fellow employee who knew his name, he'd have a kind of protective screen around him. If it was one of the security workers, even better.

But no matter what, he just couldn't wait four hours to ask Maddie for money. And he never wanted to ask her anyway. She was too special to him. He spotted red taillights up ahead and headed there quickly before another car took the space. Remember to act like you belong here, Ben told himself as he waited for a black Ford F 150 to finish pulling out.

Leaving his car unlocked, keys in the ignition, Ben walked through the automatic doors. The grey-haired greeter in the Meijer red pinny who welcomed him with a smile wasn't one Ben knew. "Can I help you find something?"

"No thank you," Ben said practicing his normal confident walk. Ben knew exactly where the electronics section was. He grabbed a cart to look like a regular shopper and walked straight through the big store past endless aisles of shelves, including the dry foods section he used to stock with Captain Crunch and headed to the back of the store.

The electronics department was fairly small and open. He hadn't remembered how brightly lit the display of computers and iPads and Fitbits was. Not good. But the sucking pain in his head didn't care. He had no choice.

"Can I help you?" a young man with a long blond hair asked as Ben stopped by the laptops. "We have the new iPod Touch that just came out in September if you're interested."

Of course Ben was interested! He was about to steal one, pay off his dealer, and get his drugs back.

"I'm just looking," Ben said pushing his empty shopping cart aside and forcing a calm tone to cover up his pounding headache.

"Cool. I'm Evan if you need any help."

Ben moved around to the iPods, turning one on and pretended to be checking it out. He waited until Evan moved over to where the television sets were. Pulling the wire clippers out of his pocket, Ben stretched his long arm to the iPod Touch section and snipped the cord attached to the closest one in the display without moving his body or head.

He edged on to the fitness watches keeping his eye on Evan. When Ben was sure Evan was not coming back and he didn't see anyone else around him, Ben circled the display table, his back to Evan, and slid the untethered white iPod into the deep pocket of his overcoat. Now all he had to do was pull the sales ticket off and stroll matter-of-factly out of the store.

"Hey," a young boy's voice said behind him as a hand touched his lower back. "You just took the same thing my daddy is buying."

Ben froze. Then he broke into a sprint toward the front of the store, consumed in panic, without even looking at the boy behind him. As he dodged grocery carts jumping in and out of aisles through the store, he recognized the sound of the store's security buzzer. Ben knew he just had to get out the door because Meijer's policy was never to chase someone into the parking lot for safety reasons.

Almost at the pharmacy near the front of the store, Ben felt a painful squeeze on his upper arm jerking him to a stop. He looked over at a burly man in a tan shirt wearing a security badge who was still pinching his biceps as a second security guard grabbed his other arm. The first guard spoke quietly with audible force in his tone, "Let's take a little walk together, Buddy."

{ 1 0 }
Promises To Keep

WEDNESDAY AUGUST 25, 2010

Pogo dropped his retrieved piece of sandy driftwood in front of Minka and Ellie where they'd paused on their beach walk, then vigorously shook water all over them both. "That felt kind of good Pogo," Ellie said patting the dog's wet head. "Cooled me off a little." Both in bathing suits, Minka and her grandmother continued walking in the cool wet sand along the Lake Michigan shoreline, Pogo loping just ahead of them.

"I'm so glad you were free to come with me this morning, Minka. I know you've been busy visiting your school friend up the road."

Minka's heart felt so heavy worrying about Andrea that, as much as she loved her grandmother, the last thing she had wanted to do this morning was take a chatty walk with her. But she just didn't have a good excuse not to.

"Why don't you bring her here sometime?"

"Who?" Minka's attention had been in Ann Arbor. "Oh, yeah, no. I can't. She has a broken leg." Minka had to smile at herself. She couldn't wait to tell Andrea that she had just made up a lie faster than Andrea could!

"I'm sorry to hear that, sweetheart," Ellie said. "Maybe when it's better she can come. And is it just me or has the sun dialed up another ten degrees?"

"It's not just you, Elliegram. That means when we get back to our beach, we're going to have to race to our flip flops because the sand's gotten so hot."

"When my feet are on fire, I can move pretty fast," Ellie said, leaning over to pick up a crushed plastic water bottle. "Look," she said as she put it in the trash bag she carried. "I'm almost full."

"Not yet," Minka said sprinting on the hot sand to pick up a silver mylar balloon dragging soggy paper ribbons.

"Nina used to complain about balloons the most," Ellie said stuffing the rumpled mylar in her bag. "The seagulls get tangled in the ribbons and can choke to death. Even drowned."

"I wish I'd known her," Minka said, thinking about how often Andrea and she had talked about Aunt Nina. Both wishing they'd known her.

"Well, you're named for her, so that's the start of knowing, Minka. And I have noticed what close attention you pay whenever we talk about her. Honey, nobody was more excited when you were born than Helena Judd. Nobody."

"Hi," they greeted two women in beach coverups walking by.

"Speaking about your being born, Minka, you haven't said much about your dad moving to Arizona. We all know how much fun you've had have the weekends he and Pat have come to see you."

When Minka didn't respond, Ellie went on, "I know you're going to miss him. But you can visit him and you'll like Tucson because the desert is so different than here," she pointed out at the water.

'If it isn't broken, don't fix it,' Andrea had said. Now her grandmother was here talking about Minka visiting Tucson and her dad was checking out schools for her there. Guilt tugged at her. Trying to decide, Minka looked over at her grandmother.

People had always said Ellie Cameron reminded them of Sophia Loren. With her olive skin and high cheekbones like Minka's Nez Perce doll, Ellie really did. But her beauty didn't matter. She could be ugly and Minka would love her just as much. Minka had no memories of life without her grandmother in it.

Even the pictures she'd colored for her when Ellie was in the hospital after a mastectomy. Their lives were entwined like the braids her grandmother had done in Minka's long hair. And it was her grandmother's unconditional love that had carried Minka through those dark times when her mother had started drinking again.

"Sweetheart," Ellie put a soft hand on Minka's tanned shoulder, "I didn't mean to upset you. I just want you to know your mom and I understand how it feels to not have a father in your life. Mine lost interest in me after my mother died and he remarried. And your mom never even got to meet her dad."

Minka walked ahead to pick up a crushed beer can and stuffed it into Ellie's bulging bag. The two walked in silence as they approached the Sandpiper's beach where their towels and flip flops lay on the sand.

"I'm sorry, Minka. I didn't mean to sound so unsympathetic because your mom and I didn't have dads either. Of course that doesn't make your dad's moving away one bit less sad for you. I was only trying to say, well, we can understand more than maybe you think we can."

If only Andrea were here. She'd know what I should say, Minka thought splashing her feet hard through the shallow water. She wished she could tell her grandmother she didn't want to talk about her dad anymore. But she didn't dare.

"Your mom and I always knew who our dads were. But you, my precocious Minka, didn't. And then you've had to grow up too fast with your mother's struggles. I think that's why you are so mature for your age. Your teachers always tell me that. You could feel sorry for yourself, but you don't. What I see, my dearest Minka, is that you've done what one of Aunt Nina's German philosophers said about hard times. What doesn't kill us makes stronger."

Minka wished she knew what Andrea was doing right now. What kind of tests she was going through. If Aunt Nina's philosopher was right, her friend had to be the strongest person Minka knew.

"I remember whenever I got into my 'my poor me' after your grandfather was killed," Ellie was saying, "Nina would cluck her tongue and tell me to think about the two wonderful daughters I had, not what I'd lost. And she'd quote her favorite Roman philosopher Cicero who said gratitude was the highest virtue."

Suddenly Minka felt anger rise in her throat. *Of course I should be grateful to have a dad at all! Andrea said the same thing! But now I'm so terrified I'm going to lose my dad or my mom that I'm not grateful for anything! You and Mom were never pulled apart by two parents,* she wanted to *yell, so Cicero can keep his stupid gratitude.*

Instead Minka took a deep breath and said, "I'm going to swim out to the second sandbar and cool off." Without waiting for an answer, she leaped through the water until it got deep enough to swim. Minka dived under the rippling waves and began doing the crawl as hard as she could. She saw Pogo start to follow her, but then turn back. She was relieved. Pogo wasn't young anymore and he knew it.

When Minka's arms finally started to ache and her lungs struggled for air, she had exercised her anger away. She headed back to the beach where Elliegram was holding Minka's towel and flip flops.

"Thank you," Minka said coming out of the water, her chest loud with heavy breathing.

"Oh, my darling First." Ellie used the special term of affection for Minka as her first grandchild. "Watching you turn into a fish before my eyes…well, I just have to tell you a story about your mom. I shouldn't because it's top secret."

"Secret from whom?" Minka asked still sucking in oxygen.

Ellie rubbed Minka's wet back and tightened the blue and pink-striped towel around her shoulders. "When I'm done, you tell me. Your mother, dear First, was the most gifted swimmer on the Spring Port High School swim team. You obviously have her genes. Watching you grace through the water just now—well, made me decide it's time to break this old secret.

"So your Aunt Kate was a nice average swimmer, and she and your mom were both on the high school swim team. Kate's senior year, Jamie was a freshman but she was the team's star swimmer who gave the school a chance to win a state title. Kate didn't qualify for state. She was the top student in her class at the same time your mom was, well, making some bad decisions. They were barely speaking.

"But then your mom found out Kate wasn't on the state roster. Mad as she could be at her big sister, that wasn't going to happen. Jamie told Coach Briggs that if Kate didn't swim at state, she wouldn't either. It was Coach Briggs, by the way, who told me this story years later. And swore me to secrecy even then. And I have kept it. Until right now."

She kissed Minka's wet head. "But seeing you swim just now with such athleticism? Well, you need to know this story."

"What happened?" Minka asked totally absorbed in what she was hearing.

"Well, according to Coach Briggs, he did everything short of threatening to kick Jamie off the team. But your mom wouldn't budge. And Briggs knew Spring Port couldn't win without Jamie. So he caved and put Kate on the state relay team. That's when your mom made him swear he would not tell anyone. Kate was never to know.

"I have a scrapbook with the news stories about your mom's incredible performance at the state championship that year. She won three single races before the final event, the relay Kate was swimming in. Your mom, Minka, swam her heart out as the relay's anchor to make sure her big sister got a medal. And the relay team not only won, but set a new state record."

Minka, her body dripping water, had stood motionless as her grandmother told the story. Her heart skidded with unexpected pride. Cameron family stories were always about Kate's successes. First Spring Port grad to get into Duke. Reporter for the Chicago Tribune. Never about Minka's mother–Jamie the alcoholic.

Ellie began using her own dry towel to rub Minka's thick wet hair. Then she paused. "You've also inherited your grandfather's coal black hair," she said, a catch in her voice. "His dark skin too. Jim never got sunburned either."

Then, as if reading her granddaughter's mind, Ellie put her hands on Minka's shivering shoulders. "Your mother is not the black sheep she thinks she is, my dear First. The other part of this story that no one, especially Kate, knows is that the state title she won on the relay helped Kate get accepted at Duke."

"I don't understand," Minka said.

"The high school counselor told Aunt Nina, who taught English there, that Kate had been wait listed by Duke before the state swim meet. When the counselor let Duke admissions know Kate had just won a state swimming title, Kate got her acceptance letter."

"So Aunt Kate got into Duke because of my mom?" Minka asked still trying to process this news.

Ellie shrugged her shoulders. "Who knows? The counselor thought so. But while Kate also had all the right grades and test scores, schools like Duke look for students who are 'well rounded' as they put it. And the timing of the acceptance letter certainly suggests your mom's amazing athletic success probably made the difference for your Aunt Kate."

As Minka followed her grandmother up the long wooden steps to the Sandpiper, she could not wait to tell Andrea what her mother had done. It would cheer Andrea up after this tough week at the University of Michigan Hospital. Andrea was going to love this story that proved Jamie Cameron wasn't the family's lost soul after all.

TUESDAY NOVEMBER 23, 2010

The Burger King was starting to fill up as Maddie again refilled her Diet Pepsi checking her watch for the zillionth time. Ben was supposed to be here an hour ago. 'He won't show up,' Gail had said. Maddie should have known anyway. She had too many memories of her mother not showing up for cleaning jobs they were supposed to do together leaving Maddie to do them by herself.

And Gail had put into words what Maddie couldn't. Ben was high or coming off something. And Maddie hadn't even told Gail about his terrible leg fracture in high school and getting hooked on pain meds. But Gail knew because of Jared. She had recognized the signs. Ben was using narcotics.

Maddie had been obsessed with the increasing number of news articles on what was now being called an 'opioid epidemic' with thousands more people dying ever year from an overdose. Gail's account of her cousin rang too true for Ben's behavior.

Even though she knew better, Maddie circled the restaurant on the wild chance she'd missed Ben coming in. With one quick look, she rounded the last booth and headed to the parking lot. She was just backing her white Subaru out when her cell rang. But it wasn't Ben's number. When she saw the caller ID, Maddie pulled back into the parking space and turned the engine off

"Will you accept a collect call from Benjamin Hughes at the Ottawa County Jail?" a male voice asked. "Ah, yes," Maddie said pressing her shoulders back against the driver's seat. After some noisy clicks on the phone line, Ben's breaking voice came on.

"Maddie. Maddie. I am such a loser," and then she heard him expel a sob.

"I'm so, oh, Maddie, no, I should never have called you." Then the crying took over.

"Hold on, Ben," Maddie said fighting her own tears. "I want to help. Please. I do. Now take some deep breaths and tell me what's going on."

Ben blew his nose and then, in a still shaky voice, told her.

"An iPod?" she couldn't disguise her shock. You stole an iPod from Meijer? Why?" she almost screamed.

"Maddie, I'm in deep trouble. Deeper than you can..." a violent wretch interrupted him.

"Ben, are you throwing up?" Maddie fought down her own gagging reflex.

After a pause, Ben said in a coughing whisper, "I've never been so sick. Ever. It's the dope."

All the pieces fell in place for Maddie, just as Gail had told her about Jared. Ben had come to her office today for money to buy heroin. But he couldn't wait four hours so he stole an iPod. And got caught.

"Maddie, Maddie, can you please, please come get me?" he asked through his sobs. "I used my one call for you because I'm not," again his voice broke, "I'm not ready to tell my parents yet."

Maddie knew she was in over her head. "Ben, I will do my best to get you out of there, but I need help to do it. Do you know for sure you're in withdrawal from...from," she could hardly say the word, "heroin? I mean has this happened before so you know?" The stone silence at the other end of the phone answered for him.

"Then you need medical support as soon as possible. Ben, I can't say when I'll be there so you'll just have to trust me."

"I'm so sick, Maddie. I've never been this bad. Not ever."

"Tell the jail you need to see a doctor immediately, Ben. I mean it. I'm hanging up now and you go make them get you medical help right now."

"Maddie...oh, Maddie." Then the jail phone clicked off.

Maddie sat, still holding the phone, unable to move. Then she touched the star on her phone and tapped one of the favorites on her phone. "Pick up, Jamie," Maddie talked out loud into her phone. "Please. Please pick up..."

"Maddie, what's up?" Jamie picked up on the fourth ring. "Whoa, whoa, Maddie," Jamie said as Maddie began speed talking. "You're going way too fast. Maddie, just calm down and tell me what you're saying. It's about Ben, right?"

Just hearing Jamie's voice soothed Maddie's stress. Jamie would know what to do. Taking a deep breath as she half saw people coming in and out of Burger King, Maddie told Ben's story. Jamie listened to the end.

"What should I do, Jamie? Could Ben die in jail from withdrawal?"

"No, no, no. He's already told you how sick he is because he's withdrawing without any medication; but he won't die. Withdrawing from alcohol can kill you if you don't get medical help, but that rarely happens coming off opioids like heroin.

"What they get instead is violently sick. Vomiting, chills and fevers, even seizures. But it's unnecessary agony so you come get me right now and we'll bail him out and get him into detox. That gives me time to get Mom here to stay with Minka and hopefully find a detox bed for Ben at the Salvation Army."

"Jamie. Please don't say anything to your mom and Casey. At least not now. Not after Gary. Casey will think I'm some kind of slut with criminal boyfriends."

"Babe," Jamie said in her mentoring tone, "I wouldn't tell them anyway because Casey would head right to the jail. He'd mean well, but this isn't the time for his help. Now get over here ASAP, Maddie."

Just over an hour later Jamie and Maddie had paid the bail, and were walking Ben through the swinging double doors of the Salvation Army's detox clinic. A short, rosy cheeked woman in a blue Salvation Army uniform came from behind the nursing station and greeted them.

"I'm Major Julia, Mr. Hughes," she said in a kindly voice as she took Ben's arm, "and we're glad to welcome you." Ben, who hadn't spoken since they left the jail, suddenly dropped his chin on his chest and silently wept.

Before Jamie and Maddie could move, Major Julia reached up to place both hands on Ben's cheeks and lifted his head to look at her. "For I know the plans I have for you, to prosper you and not to harm you, plans to give you hope and a future."

Maddie felt her eyes fill as she watched Ben fold his strong hands in prayer and bow his head. "We will take good care of Mr. Hughes, Ladies," Major Julia said, walking him down the hallway. Then looking over her shoulder, she called to them, "Remember 'All things are possible with God.'"

Maddie felt Jamie's arm around her shoulders pulling her closer as Maddie's tears rolled down her face. "All things are possible," Jamie said. Then she half chuckled and added, "I'm proof positive of that."

"Wait," a young man in a Salvation Army jacket called out as he came through the double doors behind them. "Major Julia asked me to get this to you before you left. It's from Mr. Hughes," he said holding out a folded note to Maddie who saw her name on it.

"Thank you," Maddie said taking the paper, and please thank Major Julia too."

At the jail Maddie had seen Ben's shaking hand write something while she was using her credit card to pay bail. Opening the paper, she half shouted, "No!" Jamie stopped and looked at her.

"Read this," Maddie said handing Jamie the note. "He gave us his parents' address and asked us to go tell them where he is. Jamie, it's almost ten o'clock!" Maddie said hearing the stress in her own voice.

"Why right now, Maddie? Better tomorrow when they've had a good night's sleep first."

"It's because Ben still lives with his parents. I didn't tell you because, well, he's 29 and I knew it wasn't a good sign."

"Not necessarily, Maddie. It's often a way to save money for a house or wedding. But with Ben? Not a good sign. So it looks like we have to go knock on their door as I don't see their phone number here." They walked under the great red Salvation Army shield on the building into the moonless night.

"But I do have to give Ben credit for this, Maddie," Jamie held up the note. "No parent ever wants to hear their child is in jail. Ben knew that our telling them in person would be better than a cold phone call."

As she said that, Jamie felt the familiar stab of guilt. How many times had her mother had to take such a phone call?

"Milly and Roy Hughes," Jamie read out loud as she reached the car. "I know where Union Street is. One of my friends from high school lived on that street." One of my partying friends she didn't say out loud.

"So now, Maddie, the easy part is over. Getting Ben out of jail and into detox when he was so sick? A no-brainer. But now? Telling his parents?" Neither woman spoke again until they were in the car.

"Union is off Beacon so turn right at the light," Jamie said getting in the car. "Obviously Ben used his one collect call from jail to talk to you and not them. It's a backhanded compliment, I guess, Maddie. He trusts you to do it as gently as possible."

"WE, Jamie," Maddie said pulling on her seatbelt. "You and I. You're the professional. I only met his parents once at Ben's graduation when he was still on crutches. I was just a freshman but went because I was so grateful for his going after the psycho killer Albert when he name-called me again."

"Grateful and possibly a little crush?" Jamie asked.

Maddie looked over at her passenger. "Well, if I did, so did every other girl in school."

Milly and Roy Hughes lived in a white Victorian house set back from the street with an ornamental black wrought iron fence around the front. "They're still awake," Maddie said pointing at the lighted windows.

"That is the only plus, Maddie. At least we don't have to get Mr. and Mrs. Hughes out of bed to tell them their handsome, all-state athlete son just got arrested stealing from Meijer to buy drugs because he's a heroin addict."

{ 1 2 }

Promises To Keep

FRIDAY SEPTEMBER 3, 2010

As she pedaled up the dirt road toward Andrea's cottage, Minka saw a shiny black car she'd never seen parked there before. Andrea's mother's car was always in the garage. The bright red letters on the Illinois license plate probably meant Andrea's dad was here.

Minka still hadn't met him because he only came weekends and she hadn't wanted to interfere with the limited time Andrea had with her dad. But she'd never known Mr. Armitage to drive. He always flew from Chicago to the Spring Port Municipal Airport where Andrea's mother picked him up.

"We've been looking for you, Minka," a tall, lean man with a big smile called as he came out the back door of the cottage. "I'm Brad Armitage, Andrea's father. And I'm glad to finally meet you after hearing about you all summer. You too," he said, leaning down to pet Pogo's head. "I've heard about you too."

"I'm glad to meet you too, Mr. Armitage," Minka said putting the kick-stand down on her bike by the steps to the deck. "I hope you like dogs."

"Oh, yes. Horses. Dogs. We Armitages are all big on animals. And I know this is Pogo. Andrea tells me this lug thinks he's a lap dog because he likes to lay his head on her when he's here."

Mr. Armitage waited on the deck for Minka to climb the stairs. "Now before you go see Andrea, her mother and I want to talk to you for a minute. But first we have a surprise for you. Actually, it was Andrea's idea and a good one." Reaching into the pocket of his navy sport coat, he pulled out an small white box with a new Apple iPhone inside and handed it to Minka.

"This is so you and Andrea can stay in touch." Minka stared blankly at the box for a moment before taking it out of his hand. "That is going to be very important to her from now on, Minka."

Minka heard the change in his tone and saw a twitch of pain around his bright blue eyes. She wanted to ask him a thousand questions at once about Andrea's tests in Ann Arbor. But all she could think of was, "I've never had a cell phone before. I feel like this is too much for you to give me, Mr. Armitage."

"Believe me, Minka," he said laying his hand on her shoulder, "this is for all of our family. Your time together this summer has been the best medicine she's had. When Andrea's mother tells me about all the laughing she hears…" he paused and looked toward the lake.

Then he looked straight into her eyes. "Barbara and I wanted more children, but it didn't happen. And it was hard on Andrea being the only child—especially with all her health issues. I think you, Minka, are the younger sister she always wanted. That's how she talks about you. Like she would about a little sister she adored. And she tells me how mature you are for your age. It's time you had a cell phone," he said smiling.

Then he straightened his back and gently squeezed her shoulder. "So let's go inside, Minka. Barbara wants to talk to you briefly before you see Andrea."

Pogo followed Minka into the living room overlooking Lake Michigan where Barbara Armitage jumped off the couch to greet her. "My dear Minka," Barbara Armitage said as she held out her arms, "and you too, Pogo." Minka took in the scent of gardenia sweet around Barbara at the same time she felt the tension in her body. Minka gave her a strong hug of compassion realizing she was now almost as tall as Andrea's mother.

Barbara's elegantly cut short blonde hair seemed to accentuate the tautness of her small face. She had on a cotton dress in bright pinks and orange flowers, her white strappy sandals on the floor in front of the couch where she'd been sitting.

"I heard what Brad told you, Minka. Neither of us can say enough how grateful we are for what you've meant—what you mean—to Andrea."

"But she's given me back just as much," Mrs. Armitage. "Believe me on that. And this," she held up the Apple box, "is more than you should have done. But I'll be very grateful to be able to talk to Andrea no matter where she is."

"And," Barbara Armitage said, "right now Andrea is waiting to tell you all about the testing week in Ann Arbor. You wouldn't believe how horrible it was, Minka. She wants to tell you about it herself so I won't take that away from her. But Brad and I just wanted you to know that she will probably understate the seriousness of the situation because Andrea doesn't want you to worry."

Minka's heart raced. Andrea didn't make the transplant list! Whatever happened had to be bad or she wouldn't be having this conversation with Andrea's parents.

"But I'm happy to tell you we've made an offer on this cottage because Andrea is so happy here between you and the lake. We'll get rid of all this carpet and put in wood floors, as the doctors suggested. We'll do the same in Winnetka and we're installing special air cleaners and filters in both places. They don't want her around grass cutting or vacuuming..."

"Stop, Barbara, " Brad said putting his arm around his wife. "We're interfering. This is our daughter's story to tell Minka, not ours."

Nodding her agreement, Barbara pulled a lace handkerchief out of a side pocket in her dress and wiped her wet cheeks. "You're right. All these years I've pretended Andrea's lung disease wasn't as bad as they said." Then looking right at Minka, she said, "Knowing how close you two are, I'm sure Andrea's told you that."

Then she paused. "You don't need to answer that, honey. I'm just grateful beyond words that Andrea has had you to share everything with."

"Yes. Andrea told me. But what she didn't realize was that you weren't the only one, Mrs. Armitage. I didn't believe it either–because I couldn't bear the thought it was true."

"Enough ladies," Brad pulled Minka into his other arm, "with the crying. And the confessions. I'm sure Andrea can hear us talking and she's for sure annoyed because she doesn't like to be left out of anything. And no one can lift her spirits better than you, Minka. So let's go see her."

Minka followed Mr. Armitage into a hallway she'd never been down before as he led her to an open door. "You have a special visitor, honey," he said from the doorway, waving Minka into the bedroom. "No, I mean two special visitors," he added as Pogo wagged his tail and hurried to the bed where Andrea sat propped up on silky sky-blue pillows.

"Well, it's about time, you stinker," Andrea said reaching out as Minka fell into her arms. "I heard you talking to Mom and Dad and thought you'd never get around to me."

Minka hugged her friend's shoulders as she whispered in her ear, "I've really missed you, Andrea."

Fresh tears started up again in the back of Minka's eyes as Andrea squeezed her back and quietly, seriously said, "You have no idea, my dear Minka. No idea."

Then Andrea looked over Minka's head at her father. "Thanks, Dad. I'll make sure this trouble maker doesn't spit water on me so you can close the door."

"Spit water?" he asked still holding the door open.

"I'll explain it," Nana said appearing behind him in the doorway. "So good to see you, Minka. I'll be back with a special treat in a little while," she said as she closed the door.

The room was small, the bed with four white carved posters dominating it. The two long windows overlooking the lake filled it with sunshine. Bright pink geraniums bloomed in wooden boxes below both windows.

"This could be my favorite room in this house," Minka said climbing on the foot of the bed. "But you don't need to tell me how much you'd rather be out there, Andrea," she pointed at the window, "than in here."

As Minka seated herself cross-legged, eye level with Andrea, she told herself the slight bluish tint in her friend's lips was just a reflection from the pillows. All she really wanted to know was if Andrea qualified for the transplant list. She'd been too afraid to ask the Armitages. Wouldn't they have told her right away if she was on it? Now Minka was even more afraid to come out and ask Andrea. Trying to smile, Minka forced a casual tone. "Now I have to know everything that happened at the hospital, Andrea."

Andrea gave Minka her signature upbeat grin, and in a breathy voice said, "Well, for starters, how about four days of being poked with needles," she pushed up the long sleeve on her navy shirt to show the clusters of bruising. "Oh, and you haven't even said anything about my new U of M shirt yet!" She patted the big yellow M on the front of her tee shirt. "Guess why I picked out this one?"

"You did not!" Minka fired back.

"Oh, yes I did. And I have one for you too so we both can wear "M" for Minka shirts when you come visit me."

"Come visit you?" Minka's voice rose. "Does that mean what I hope hope it does? I can't stand it any longer, Andrea. Are you on the list?"

"Silly, you! I'd have yelled it out when I heard you coming in the door today if I were."

"Does that mean you didn't make it?" Minka gasped as she leaned forward toward Andrea.

"Goofy! I'd have told you that too, my Minka of many questions. No. I'm still waiting to hear from the OPTN–I've learned several fancy new acronyms at U Hospital–that's what they call the Michigan hospital. The Organ Procurement Transplantation Network meets regularly to review all the patients in the country who need an organ transplant."

Andrea paused, "And there are thousands and thousands of us. That's why they have to prioritize all of us by age and severity of disease and chances of survival. Organs are so hard to come by, they have to do it.

"So I still don't know if I'm on the list for lungs. But now that this OPTN has my test results they said I could hear any time now. I mean have you ever seen me have a cell phone right next to my hand before?" she patted the one beside her on the bed.

"One call from U Hospital and it's either," she pointed her thumbs up, "or," she pointed her thumbs down. Then she broke into her irresistible giggle. "But before I tell you anything else, you need to tell me why we want thumbs down!"

"You jerk! You have me scared to death and then you make me take a stupid quiz before you tell me about Ann Arbor. You're impossible," Andrea. "Of course I want a thumbs down just like every gladiator in the Colliseum did! Throw 'down' your arms and let this gladiator live. So now will you please finish about your transplant testing?"

"Good job on the Roman history, Minka," Andrea said. Then, pointing at her, she said, "Sorry, but first you need to tell me about your dad and mom. I can't be worrying about you while I'm trying to talk about four days of being examined like an invasive species."

Minka threw up her hands in surrender. "I know what extortion means and I just heard it. So you chicken dinner me again. But then you do have to tell me everything!"

"I swear. On Pogo's Honor," Andrea raised one hand in a pledge sign, the other on Pogo's head where it rested beside her on the bed.

"That feels kind of sacrilegious Andrea, but I'll take it. So I have followed your advice and not said a word to my mom about dad's talking up Tucson and living with him there. I came close to telling Elliegram last summer while we were beach walking." Then she grabbed Andrea's leg where it lay on the bed. "But I could just hear you yelling at me so I kept my mouth shut."

"I'd more than yell at you, Minka. The time for talking about it will come, but not before it has to. So he keeps bringing up Tucson and your mom doesn't know it. That is still best for now. Any other updates I should know?"

Minka shook her head with a little chuckle. "You are truly spooky, sometimes, Andrea. Like you always know what I want to say and then say it for me. But it's creepy you asked me this extra question. Good creepy, mind you. But still creepy."

"I love good creepy, M. Go!"

"Andrea, I've been waiting to tell you a really happy story about my mom that happened when she was a freshman at Spring Port High School. Elliegram told me my mom didn't want anyone to know about it because of how it might hurt my Aunt Kate. So Mom made the only two people who did know promise to keep it a secret. The swim coach was one and Elliegram was the other."

Telling the story of the state swimming championship, Minka could see Andrea's eyes twinkle as she listened intently. When Minka finished with the relay win, Andrea clapped her hands and smiled with her whole face. "And your mother didn't ever want her sister to know because it would take away from Kate's success getting into Duke." She paused to take some deep breaths.

"So, Minka, of course I wish your mom didn't have a drinking problem. But what you just told me about her says something that far outweighs it. She has character. Grit. I know now where you get it from, my dear young friend. And for sure I need to meet your mom some day."

Pogo nudged Andrea's hand on the bed. "Yes, Pogo," she stroked his greying head, "you have character too."

Minka hopped off the bed and handed Andrea a water glass with a straw in it. "You sound like you need some water. And I can't wait any longer so you need to drink before you start talking."

Andrea looked over the glass at Minka as she sipped through the straw. "I did need that," she said handing the glass back. "You always know what I'm thinking too, M. I think I like that little name M for you. It goes with our shirts."

"And how about the James Bond movies too? You're Bond so I can be your boss M!"

Andrea made a sputtering giggle that got Minka laughing too. "Of course you'd think of that, M. Especially the part about my working for you!"

A light tap on the door and Nana came in with a tray carrying two bowls of peppermint ice cream on an Oreo crust covered with fudge sauce and a pitcher of ice water and glasses. She set it down on the table beside Andrea's bed, handing each girl a bowl.

"You see how they're really trying to fatten me up since we got back from Ann Arbor, Minka. But, Nana," Andrea said taking a big spoonful, "this could be your best dessert trick yet."

"Your mom made it, darling. And I'm rather afraid I am the one who is getting fattened up. Isn't it delicious?"

"I never ate anything this good," Minka said carefully dabbing chocolate off her mouth with a napkin.

"Good. Then I'm glad I interrupted you two. Until that last outburst I just heard, you were being way too quiet for your usual selves! But now I'll scoot while you two eat your ice cream."

When they were done, Minka put their empty dishes on the tray and climbed back on the bed. She looked directly into Andrea's deep blue eyes and waited.

Andrea began almost in a monotone. "You saw the bruise marks from the first day when they took 14 vials of blood to run every test you can do on a human being. What I didn't know was those blood draws would be the easy part!

"By far the worst was the spirometer testing of my pulmonary function. I'm in a glass box that looks like a phone booth with this plastic tube in my mouth connected to a spirometer. 'Spiro' is Latin for 'breathe,' by the way—since we're into Rome today."

Minka stuck her tongue out at Andrea.

"Well that was mature, Ms. M." Andrea said sticking her tongue out too.

"So now in this phone booth with the tube in my mouth, I have to tighten my lips so it's air tight. Then they put a plastic clothes pin on my nose so I can't cheat and breathe through my nose. Try it and see what it feels like."

Minka pinched her nose with two fingers, and pursed her lips taking several deep breaths. "It's hard for me."

"Thank you for saying that, my friend," Andrea smiled. "So then it's breathe in, breathe out, hold my breath—at one point it felt like my heart would explode out of my chest."

"When I'm out of breath like that from swimming too hard, I just quit. And you couldn't!"

"I wanted to, believe me. But they needed to measure how much air I inhale and exhale and how long it takes. Then they measured the oxygen and carbon dioxide in my blood. That was much easier."

Andrea leaned back to take some deep breaths. "Then a six minute walk to test how far these," she patted her chest, "could take me. Then three hours with catheters in my heart, and something called a VQ scan which is more than you need to know–and more than my shortness of breath wants to talk about." Andrea made huffing sound as she took a huge inhale of breath.

"So what did the doctors at U Hospital tell you after all these tests, Andrea?" Minka had many more questions to ask, but Andrea's stressed breathing forced her to be calm.

Then Andrea's sudden giggle scared Minka while it made her smile at the same time. To think she could lose that laughter in her life terrified Minka. But for this moment it was okay because her best friend was happy.

"You impatient funny bunny, M. Your new name now," Andrea touched the front of her navy Michigan shirt. "No more questions now. Go look in my closet over there," she pointed at a closed door. "Yours is hanging right in front."

"Andrea, your dad just gave me an iPhone, as you know," Minka said getting off the bed. "No more presents after this or I'll have to give you something."

"Feel free, M! I love presents," Andrea said watching Minka pull the navy tee shirt over her heard. "It is the right size! Good. We're twinners."

"Go Blue!" Minka said patting the M on her shirt.

"But, Andrea," she said sitting back on the bed, "you didn't say anything about the personal questions I know they had to ask. And, yes, it's my last question because I can see you're tired. I don't want you to spend too much oxygen talking to me so just the short version?"

Andrea took a big inhale before she answered. "They need to make sure I'm emotionally stable enough because, well, because putting new lungs in someone's chest is…you don't need me to spell it out. The big fear will always be rejection, and they need to make sure I can handle that. Donor lungs are the hardest organs to come by so they want them to go to the best candidates.

"They spent hours with my parents and me to make sure we truly understand what happens after the surgery and are committed to the aftercare. You've met my parents and my grandmother. The problem will be their over-doing it!"

Minka smiled as she patted Andrea's leg. "Yes, I can see that! And the one test I know you passed with flying colors is emotional stability. With all you've been through growing up, Andrea, you're so steady. In fact you'd be boring if you weren't so smart and funny and kind…"

"Stop already. My head's swelling. And because it's you, I have to be honest. Thinking about rejection if I even get the lungs–well, does scare me." Andrea paused for a moment. "But let's not go there now."

Pogo came back to the bed, laying his head between them as they both petted him. "Dogs know, don't they?" Andrea asked. "When we're in deep waters. Now don't you dare cry on me, Minka! I mean it," she said forcing her tone up.

"Oh, Andrea. I came here hoping you'd tell me you didn't need a transplant–and now I'm praying hard as I can you're on the list so you can get new lungs!" Minka wiped her eyes on her sleeve.

"That's why you have the cell phone, Minka. You need to be with me from now on. And I need to be there for you when your mom finds out what your dad's been telling you. I need you to have a phone so I can call as soon as I hear if I'm on the list. And then, God willing," she looked up at the ceiling, "to call you the minute I have a donor."

"Oh, I want that just as much, Andrea. But I don't want anyone to know I have a cell. They'd ask questions and I'm not ready to tell them about you yet."

"You just put it on vibrate," she showed Minka the button on the side of her iPhone. Just keep it in a pocket. And Dad is leaving the heat and internet on here so you can come any time to call me. That way no one will hear you talking about your parents. Dad put the cottage's entry code in your phone already and our caretaker Bruce knows you'll be here sometimes.

"Hey, no crying, M. You'll make me cry and you know that's hard on my breathing. The last thing we have to talk about is what neither of us wants to." Andrea leaned back, closing her eyes for a moment before she continued. "Even if I'm lucky enough to get on the list, which is a big 'if,' someone has to die for me to get new lungs."

Neither of the girls moved in the suddenly quiet room. Finally Minka nodded slowly.

"And so many things have to be compatible, blood types for starters. If I'm on the list, I have to have my cell on me 24/7 so when my donor dies the hospital will call me and I have to go there immediately. I need to keep my suitcase packed. But just think how lucky I am M. My dad has his own plane so he can get me from Chicago to Ann Arbor in barely an hour."

Minka put her head down on Andrea's outstretched legs and wept as Pogo put his head next to hers. "Only you, Andrea. Only you would say that."

"But I am lucky, M. I have you as my closest friend." Outside the sound of seagulls swirled in the air as the two friends stayed silent, Andrea's hand stroking Minka's black hair .

Suddenly the phone beside Andrea lit up. "University of Michigan Hospital" caller ID. The two girls were still just staring at the phone when Andrea's parents burst into the room holding their own ringing phones.

"Yes, this is," Andrea inhaled as she finally answered. The sound of rolling waves outside filled the stilled room. Minka sat motionless holding her breath.

"Yes. Yes, I will. Thank you." Suddenly Minka let out a war whoop. While Andrea was still on the phone, she had held out her free hand with the thumb pointed down.

{ 13 }

Promises To Keep

WEDNESDAY NOVEMBER 17, 2010

Minka barely waited for Andrea to pick up the phone before she started talking to her. "**Unbroken** is the hardest book I have ever had to read, Andrea." Minka sat on the soft leather lounge chair in the living room of the Armitage's cottage, her feet on the footstool, Pogo curled up close to the fireplace beside her.

"I told you that ahead of time, M." Andrea answered, her voice steady, but weak. "And, yes. You're right. It's very tough reading. And I think you know why I asked you—you did not *have* to—read it–don't you?"

"I knew when I read the back cover, Andrea. You weren't very subtle I must say."

"And?"

"If Louis Zamperini can survive being shipwrecked in the ocean for 40 some days and then two-and-a-half years of torture by a sadistic Japanese guard, you can survive a double lung transplant."

Andrea paused to take some audible breaths. "We Scorpios are known for our honesty, M. We both know I'm not getting any better. But reading **Unbroken** helped me put my stress in perspective. My operation and post-surgery pain will not last for years like his suffering did.

"But you know what I got out of **Unbroken** I hadn't expected, M? That a man heroic enough to survive almost three years of suffering and brutality could then give in to alcohol? It told me something about your mother. It doesn't matter how strong you are. If you are alcoholic, the drink is still stronger."

Andrea's words warmed Minka's heart as she felt a new compassion and pride for her mother.

"But the more important part, my M," Andrea continued, "is that Zamperini did get sober and never drank again. And your mom's doing the same! The story you told me about her? She's got Zamperini's same kind of courage to stay sober."

Minka stared into the flames of the gas-driven fireplace absorbing every word she was hearing on the phone. Then, as she looked out at the tumultuous roiling waves in the Big Lake, she wondered how she could ever get along without Andrea in her life.

"Thank you for that, Andrea. Remember when we were reading Emily Dickinson because she was Aunt Nina's favorite poet? 'Hope is a thing with feathers.' I think it's what keeps us both going."

"I know it does, M. And I think that's part of why God sent you down our dirt road last summer. Speaking of the cottage, is everything working? Water? Heat?"

"My bad, Andrea. I forgot to tell you I finally met Bruce. I heard a truck and when I opened the back door, he just asked if the heat was okay and did I need anything. Then he walked around the house and left."

"That's so Bruce. He took good care of us all summer, but always so quietly you hardly ever got to see him. But trust me, he's watching out for you M. So let's talk about you. I'm assuming everyone still thinks you're on an after-school dog walk when you go to our cottage."

"And it's never a lie because I do. They don't need to know the part about coming here so I can call you. Pogo gets a good walk and I get a nice bike ride. And I can keep riding until the snow gets too deep."

"And I have to tell you, Minka," Andrea said in a serious tone, "I don't think I could have made it these past months waiting for a donor call without our daily chats to look forward to." Andrea took a breath and, now half laughing, said, "I think my parents and Nana appreciate your calls just as much because they know I'll be in a good mood afterwards."

"It's the same for me," Minka scratched Pogo's head. "You help me stop worrying about what will happen with my dad and mom. And Pogo knows I'm talking to you right now because he just got up and put his head on my lap."

"Oh, I miss him too. So now your dad is moving in a few weeks. Any thing new today?"

"No. But I think something's happening next week when I'm on Thanksgiving break. He's taking me out for lunch the day after and then wants to talk to Mom alone. She's usually glad for me to have time with him–but you and I know she wouldn't be if she knew about the Tucson talk. Anyway, I could tell she wasn't happy that he wants to meet with her alone after our lunch. I'm supposed to go to Elliegram's until they're done."

"Whoa," Andrea said. "This does sound serious. And I am guessing you will not go to your grandmother's."

Minka made a clucking sound with her tongue. "You know very well I'll be tucked into some good listening post at our cabin. I'll need to come up with a good story about why I didn't go to my grandmother's. But I can lie almost as well as you now. Hey, I forgot to tell you how fast I came up with one last summer when Elliegram asked why the friend I kept visiting never came to our beach. I told her you had a broken leg!"

Andrea tried to answer before a coughing giggle took over. "That only proves what a good teacher I've been," she finally could say.

"Or what a good student I have been. And now it's my turn to pick out a book so we're going to read **The Hunger Games** next."

"Isn't that the novel about teenagers hunting each other down to kill them? You know I'm not big on science fiction–and really not a fan of violence, M."

"And who didn't want to read **Unbroken**? My friend Maddie says **The Hunger Games** is a great page-turner and so is the sequel **Catching Fire**. And a third one just came out. "

Now Andrea laughed openly into the phone. "Hold on! Let's just start with the first one and then decide. I'll ask Mom to get **The Hunger Games** at the library tomorrow. A page-turner doesn't sound too bad, actually, M." Andrea paused and took a deep breath. "I'm obsessively wanting this blasted phone to ring and then scared to death it will."

Minka pulled out the rabbit's foot and rubbed it against her cheek. "Remember the rabbit's foot Tommy gave me?"

"For good luck after you fell off his tramp."

"Well, I'm holding it right now for your phone call. And when it does ring, who wouldn't be afraid? And I'd rather you didn't say 'scared to death,' my very smart friend."

"Bad word choice, Minka. Terrible actually. But since 'death' came up un-intentionally, there's a poem I've wanted to talk to you about since I came back to Chicago from Ann Arbor. On one of those long days when I was being tested at U Hospital, I found a newsletter about highlights in the University of Michigan's history. Kennedy announced the Peace Corps there. Jonas Salk did research just before he developed the polio vaccine. But what I liked best was that Robert Frost moved to Ann Arbor in 1920 to become the University of Michigan's first artist in residence."

"My English teacher Mrs. Fowler loves Frost," Minka said. "But she didn't say–maybe didn't know–he ever lived in Michigan. His poems are about New England. "

"Vermont where he lived. But what really grabbed me about this article on Frost is that the one poem that has touched me most closely since my diagnosis he actually wrote when he lived in Ann Arbor! *Stopping by the Woods on a Snowy Evening*. It blew my mind to find out he wrote this poem about death within miles of the hospital where I was getting tested for new lungs to keep me from dying."

Minka took a moment to respond. "We read it in Mrs. Fowler's class, and I don't like hearing you talk about a death poem."

"But, M, that's the point. In the end, Frost says he's not ready to die because he has 'miles to go' before he sleeps.

"Are you still there?' Andrea asked when Minka didn't say anything.

"Andrea. That's pretty heavy stuff you just said."

"I know. And I've wanted to tell you before. But it was just too morbid to bring up. I only did now because I'd used the 'death' word myself. Probably a Freudian slip. But now I'm glad I did because that poem–what it means to me is something I can't talk to my family about. None of them has ever talked about what could happen.

"I try not to think about it either. But this Frost poem? How random that I found out it was written near the Michigan transplant hospital? And, M, it did for me what you just talked about. It gave me 'the thing with feathers.' A positive way to think about the transplant. I'm not ready for 'sleep' either because I have miles to go before then. And, M, I have 'promises to keep.' Oh, please don't cry, M. Frost gives me words to hang on to. That's a God thing."

Minka wiped at her eyes and strained to keep her voice steady. "You have to keep your promises to me, Andrea."

"Stop it right now, Minka. I can hear you crying and if you get me started, you'll mess up my breathing. More than it already is."

After a moment, Minka said more evenly, "Now I'm going to have to go find my book from Mrs. Fowler's class and see if I wrote any notes by this poem."

"Tell me if you did. And it's getting close to dinner time where you are so you better get going. No more tears, Minka. And since I have to keep my phone on my person at all times, I expect my best friend to do the same."

Then she took a big breath in. "It's weird, M, but knowing you're waiting for it to ring too makes me feel less alone. That's pretty selfish, isn't it?"

"We're soul mates, remember, Andrea? Determined Scorpios born to have great friendships. There's no such thing as selfish between us. You give me a security no one else can. So I better be doing the same for you.

"My phone's on vibrate 24/7. No one in my family still knows I have a cell so they can't ask me where I got it. It's on my pillow at night and in my pocket all day. And you better call me fast!"

"You will be my first and only call, Minka. My parents will get their own calls. Oops. I hear my mother coming with my endless pills. Come on in, Mom," Andrea said away from the phone.

"That is unless," she whispered back to the phone, "I get a donor call tonight like the one that came about the transplant list when you were right beside me? Wouldn't that be a nice birthday present for us?"

Not just nice, but the best birthday present I could ever get in my whole life, Minka thought. "Yes it would, my best ever Scorpio."

MID-MORNING FRIDAY
NOVEMBER 26, 2010

Minka headed north on the beach into the chilling November wind so she could walk back with the wind behind her. She'd always tried to get the hard stuff done first—like geometry homework with a protractor so then she could read some good short stories for English. She bent her head into the snow-flakes as Pogo walked beside her, his eyes blinking against the blowing sand.

Her dad was picking her up in an hour, and she had to have her plan ready. She'd already made sure to wear the white North Face coat Pat and he had given her. At the same time she'd pushed her Michigan "M" shirt to the back of her closet where her mom wouldn't see it. Minka had no good lie about where it came from.

Pogo turned around when they reached their usual mid-point at the sand dune where a movie with Tom Hanks had been filmed. Now the wind at their backs helped propel the two forward as Minka thought about this coming lunch with her dad. Minka knew she couldn't let him start talking about Tucson again—how much she'd like it there. She had to get him on a different topic. Walking back over her own boot marks in the sand, Pogo's paw prints beside hers, she'd figured it out.

An hour later Minka was out the door of the log cabin at the first sound of a car in the driveway. She knew her dad didn't want to see her mother yet and her mother didn't want to see him. Minka had to protect them both.

"Don't you look nice, Minka," Keith said as she got into his car. I'll bet you've been walking Pogo in this wind because your cheeks have a nice rosy color."

"Yup. On the beach. And I was warm with this nice coat you and Pat gave me for my birthday."

"It looks nice." Then as he waited for her to put on her seatbelt, he added, "But you'd never need that coat in Ariz…"

"Oh, sorry," Minka cut him off, "to interrupt, but I have something really important to tell you about a friend of Maddie's. Maddie wants your professional advice." Minka's first lie of the day. But not the last. And even if Maddie hadn't asked, Minka knew how much she respected Dr. Keith Summers and would listen to any advice he'd have about Ben.

Minka stuck to her plan, dragging out every detail from when Ben was a star football player in high school, three years older than Maddie, to how he shoved a disturbed student into the lockers when he bullied Maddie. The secret crushes Maddie and Ben had had on each other.

Her dad already knew about Maddie's friendship with the murdered Russian pawnbroker and how she'd solved the crime. So Minka couldn't carry on about that. Instead she went into great detail about Ben's terrible fracture as Spring Port's star running back. The pain killer dependency that became a heroin addiction. And she embellished Ben's story the rest of the way into Spring Port.

"Well, here we are," Keith Summers said as he parked in front of the Wharf. It was the restaurant where seven years before Joe and Gloria had set him up to 'run into' Jamie–and then to find out he had a daughter. "This is a very special place to me, Minka," he said. "I'll tell you about it one of these days."

Minka barely ate her hamburger because as soon as her dad answered another of her questions about addiction, she'd ask something else. "So how long does detox take? Where does Ben go after that? How is his heroin addiction different than my mother's alcoholism?"

Finally her dad put his head back and started laughing. "You were a chatterbox the first time I took you kayaking, Minka. But you've outdone yourself today, my darling daughter."

Minka winced. She was his daughter and she loved him as much as she loved her mother. But she couldn't let him start a conversation about kayaking when they first met. Or how overjoyed he felt finding out he had a child. How she'd become the most important thing in his life. All the reasons she should move to Tucson with him and spend her summers and vacations with her mother.

"Do you remember the day…" he began. But Minka was so tired of trying to distract him that this time she just listened. And fought down the awful guilt rising inside as she knew her silence was a betrayal. She could have told her mother her dad wanted her to move to Arizona with him. But Andrea had been right. These past few months Minka had loved spending time with her dad, ignoring the talk about Tucson the best she could—and never mentioning a word of it to her mother.

But what if that was why he wanted to talk to her mother alone today? What would her mother say? How would she feel that Minka had never told her? As they drove back to log cabin talking about the Christmas decorations already up, Minka needed to talk to Andrea. She felt the silenced cell phone in her jeans pocket and wanted to call Andrea right now. No one else would understand her fear—feeling more like terror every minute they got closer to the cabin.

*   *   *

Jamie nervously cleaned up the kitchen counter and checked her watch again. Minka and Keith had been gone since 12:11. She'd made sure of the exact time, and now it was 1:25. Jamie wished she hadn't needed to take Antabuse again. That her sobriety was strong enough to tough it out like Gloria wanted her to no matter what Keith had to say. But more than that, Jamie was grateful that she had taken it and it was working. One drink could kill her.

She turned on the coffee and wiped off the darkened old pine kitchen table. Jamie wanted to believe the table's stains had been made by her parents in the few days they'd had together in this honey-colored log cabin before Captain James Cameron was shipped to Vietnam.

For Jim and Ellie Cameron, like Dickens, those days had been the best of times and the worst of times. Deliriously happy just being together here with their little Katie. Abysmally sad as the hours counted down before he had to leave. And complicating it all was Jamie herself. A baby growing in Ellie that James Cameron knew nothing about.

Ellie's plan to have a baby so the new Dr. Cameron wouldn't go to Vietnam hadn't worked. In the end, she realized volunteering for Vietnam was something he had to do. Aunt Nina, as always, had been right. The day Aunt Nina met Ellie at the Sandpiper, she told Ellie to let Jim go.

"The man you love has to do this," Aunt Nina had said. "Because that is who he is—and why you love him." Not until the night Dr. Cameron flew out to Vietnam, did Ellie tell him he would have a second child when he came back. But he didn't come back.

Jamie had the cabin door open before Keith and Minka were out of the car. Seeing them together, looking so natural as a father and daughter, made Jamie press both hands on her belly to push down the nausea.

Minka wasn't surprised to see the log cabin door open as she and her dad pulled in the driveway. Her mother had been waiting for them, probably looking out the window.

Getting out of the car, Minka saw the tight muscles around her mother's mouth matched by her stiff posture. Minka felt the tension in the air like a heightened blast of frigid air. "Hello, Jamie," her dad said in a different voice, but one Minka recognized. He was now Dr. Summers, the clinician, the objective scientist. He'd used the same tone answering all her questions about Ben.

Following her dad through the door her mother held open, Minka could feel the anxiety between her parents. "I know you two want to talk alone. But before I go to Elliegram's, I'm running to the beach and," she said pulling a thick blue mitten out of her jacket pocket, "looking for my other one."

Then she stepped hard on the cabin's wooden floor making heavy feet sounds going to her bedroom where she quickly took her boots off before yelling goodbye. Then she slammed the back door, but stayed inside. In her quiet stocking feet, she tiptoed to the hall closet, tucking herself into the space she'd cleared the day before.

EARLY FRIDAY AFTERNOON
NOVEMBER 26, 2010

"Looks like you two had a nice lunch together, Keith." Jamie couldn't help noticing Keith looked younger than his 50s, his dark hair barely tipped with white. Immaculately dressed in his V-necked navy sweater and khakis, Keith could play the perfect father in a TV series. "Did you get your run in this morning?" she forced her tone to sound calm. Neutral.

"A couple miles on the track at the high school. It's close to the motel. You?"

"Same old Lakeshore loop," Jamie said as evenly as she could. "I miss running with Kate, though…" Jamie almost said something about Kate's seven-year old twins not giving their mother much free time to run. But she caught herself. Children were the last thing she wanted to bring up right now. "I made coffee," she said leading him into the kitchen.

Keith's smile as he thanked her reminded Jamie of how much she had liked him. But it wasn't enough. For her or for him. She tried to keep her hand steady as she poured coffee in two Sandpiper Foundation mugs, again grateful the Antabuse was in her blood stream. She didn't offer sugar or cream. She knew he only drank it black.

"Seems your Wolverines are looking for a new football coach," Keith said as he took the coffee.

"I guess so," Jamie replied, glad to put off what she dreaded was coming. I'm not really a big football fan."

"They don't like Rodriguez's record."

"Didn't they just hire him?" Jamie knew the answer but needed stalling time.

"Yes. He took Carr's place so this is his third year."

Then, as uncomfortable silence filled the kitchen, Jamie felt silly about this too obvious small talk. "Keith," she blurted out, "enough of this. Tell me why you're here."

Keith's shoulders rose as he audibly expelled lungs full of air and looked out the window up toward The Sandpiper. Then he leaned back and tented his hands on the table in the posture Jamie vividly remembered when he was her psychiatrist at the Saguaro Rehabilitation Clinic twelve years before. It struck her that this was also a gesture of prayer. She already felt prayed out.

Jamie clenched her fists under the table. "We both know we're putting off why you wanted to talk to me alone." Jamie felt her cheeks flare with a flush.

Keith studied his hands a moment longer before raising his head to look straight at Jamie. "Has Minka said any thing to you about Tucson?" Keith asked now in his professional, clinical voice.

"Yes. That she's very sorry you're moving there because it's so far away and she won't have weekends with you anymore. But I've told her how much I liked the desert even living in a rehab clinic. That she'd have fun visiting you there. So what do you need to talk about, Keith?"

Keith sat still, again studying his hands. "Jamie, I've thought about this all summer. The day you told me I was that bright little girl's father was the happiest day of my entire life. Bar none. These past seven years spending time with her, watching her grow from a chatty child into a precocious, sensitive 12-year-old." He paused.

"To not have her in my life was unthinkable to me. Is unthinkable. But I didn't do anything about it. I couldn't do it. Take my daughter…"

"Our daughter, Keith," Jamie snapped. "Ours! And what do you mean 'take'?"

"Jamie, you have to know I have lost sleep worrying about how hard it would be on you if Minka came with Pat and me to Arizona. That's why I fought this so long. But, Jamie, Minka is the only child I'll ever have. Pat is too old to have children and you're still young enough to have more."

Jamie's stomach churned. He was saying everything but the word she had been dreading. "You don't replace a child by having another one, Keith!" Jamie yelled at him. "There's only one Minka!"

"That came out wrong, Jamie," Keith shook his head. "I'm sorry. I didn't mean it that way. Of course you can't. That's just why I'm hoping we can work something out, some arrangement that gives you lots of time with her but gives me legal custody..."

"NO!" Jamie screamed so loud her own ears rang.

"My lawyer is ready to ask for full custody, but he won't do anything until I say so. He agrees with me that you and I should be able to work this out our-selves–especially knowing we're both mental health professionals. He doesn't want the court to decide any more than I do."

Jamie felt like she'd been turned to stone. The snake-headed witch in Aunt Nina's mythology stories had turned Jamie's body into a petrified fossil. Jamie could barely move her eyes to see Keith looking down, his head drooped in sadness.

"Jamie, this is the most painful thing I've ever had to do in my whole life." Keith sat motionless, his head still down as the honking of geese flying south filled the quietness. Then he looked right at her, his lips a hard straight line. In his low, physician's voice, he said, "Jamie, you are a single mother and we're all proud of your recovery but–and for me of all people to say this is profoundly painful–you still have a history of alcoholism..."

Suddenly the cement broke open and she screamed, "You hypocrite!" cutting him off as she smacked the table so hard the mugs jiggled. "You the big author of the book teaching the world that alcoholics have a brain disease. We are not evil!" her voice reverberating against the logs.

"Bullshit!" Jamie spit out her words. "You go out and tell your audiences we alcoholics can be saved from relapses by telling ourselves we're not losers... and now you use my relapse history as a reason to try and steal Minka from me!" Jamie felt the hot tears running down her face.

Keith, still in his psychiatrist's voice, said, "Pat and I can provide a stable home as a married couple. And you know as well as I do how much Minka and Pat like each other. Even love. I know Pat loves her."

Jamie couldn't find words. It was true. You couldn't help liking Pat. Gentle and kind, Pat had been Keith's PR person for the book tour selling **Rewrite or Relapse**. She'd often come with him to Spring Port to see Minka. Pat and Keith had gotten married three months ago.

"I suppose it's a coincidence you two got married just before you decided to ask for custody?" Jamie squeezed the sides of her face as saying the word sent shock waves through her brain.

Keith opened his hands in the gesture of helplessness. "Why don't we let Minka decide and no lawyers or court involved?"

Jamie couldn't hold back a gasp. "Tell me you didn't just say that, Keith.

Tell me you didn't say Minka should choose! You a psychiatrist asking a 12-year-old to make such a decision! To cut off her left arm or her right?"

"Jamie, Jamie," Keith spoke as if to a child, "Minka would come back every summer and for Christmas and any other special occasions. I'll always do that. And pay for her flights."

"So now you're throwing the money angle at me! Because you're a best-selling writer and head of an exclusive rehab and I'm a part-time counselor helping troubled teens with no insurance! I'm sure the judge will like your finances better than mine...but holy shit, Keith. You know her life is here! With her mother and grandmother and Kate and Pete and for God's sake Maddie and the twins and Pogo.

"That's why she's there right now," Jamie pointed out the window at the Sandpiper. "That's 'our' daughter's happy place. And that lake out there," Jamie jabbed her finger toward Lake Michigan," her voice trembling, "it's been part of who she is since she was born. You kayak with her. You know what the Big Lake means to her."

Keith stood up abruptly. "I know she loves to swim and I told her our new house has a swimming pool and a riding stable near by and an excellent private school near us."

Almost too stunned to speak, Jamie leaned toward Keith half spitting out the words, "What did you say?" Jamie "What did you just say?" she repeated in a shocked tone.

"And now you're saying you already told her about a swimming pool and horses and now a new mom and probably next a new dog! You heartless bastard," Jamie dug her fingernails into her palms. "I'd smack you right now if I didn't know you'd report it as more evidence against me."

Keith picked up his mug and walked slowly to the kitchen sink, taking his time rinsing it out before he turned around. "I can't tell you how sorry I am, Jamie." His voice cracked as he went on. "That you and I who want what's best for our daughter can't agree on what that is. So now we have to put it on her to decide." Keith shook his head. "Terrible, terrible for her."

"Please Keith, don't do this. Please. You can have her in the summer and whatever vacations you want, but she belongs here."

Keith looked up at the ceiling as tears filled his eyes. "My lawyer made an appointment with the Friend of the Court here in case you and I couldn't do this together. He did it because it can take a long time to set up a meeting and I'm leaving in just a few weeks. I'll call you with the date and details."

As Keith took his coat off a hook by the front door and left, Jamie collapsed into her chair burying her face into her arms folded on the table. She didn't hear the back door open a few minutes later as Minka stepped into her winter boots, pulled on her backpack filled with a change of clothes and toiletries, and headed to the shed where she kept her bike.

Minka knew where she had to go and with only a light dusting of snow, it was easy to peddle. With one hand in her pocket, she furiously rubbed the rabbit's foot Tommy had given her after she gashed her ankle jumping off his trampoline. 'You always do that crazy kind of stuff, Minka,' Tommy had said crossly when he handed her the good luck keychain saying she needed it.

Tommy had been her best friend growing up. Two years older than she was, Tommy had been the one who'd named her Minka when he couldn't pronounce her real name Helena. Tommy could never stay mad at Minka.

Minka always put the rabbit's foot in her pocket when she was afraid. And she'd been scared this morning. Her mother had been so jumpy waiting for Minka's dad to come. She could tell something bad was going to happen. But Minka could not have imagined how bad. She rubbed the rabbit's foot and suddenly, as if the magic luck had worked already, Pogo appeared, loping beside her as he always did.

Minka felt the tears cold on her cheeks pedaling her bike as she and Pogo headed for the cottage Andrea had left open for her. Only Andrea would have known how much Minka would need an escape hatch. By the time they reached the dirt road leading to the Armitage's cottage, Minka's tears had turned into hurtling sobs.

{ 1 6 }

Promises To Keep

LATE AFTERNOON FRIDAY
NOVEMBER 26, 2010

"What do you mean she's not there?" Jamie asked her mother on the phone, too drained of emotion to really think about what she was asking.

"Honey," Ellie said, "I haven't seen Minka since I waved at her coming up from the beach before she went out for lunch. "And I've been worried all afternoon about what Keith wanted to talk to you about. But I knew you'd call when you were ready."

Whatever slim hold Jamie had on her emotions crashed when she heard her mother's voice. "Keith, Keith wants," Jamie said through choking tears, "custody so, so he can take her to Tucson with him." Jamie covered her face with a paper napkin already soaked with tears.

"Oh, darling," Ellie said. "I'm coming there right now."

"Wait, Mom. First I need to figure out where Minka is. She was coming to stay at your house while Keith was here. Now I see why he didn't want her here. He didn't want her to hear that he wants full custody, and she should decide which parent to live with or the court would." Jamie wiped her face with her sleeve.

"Oh, my God, Jamie! Nothing would be crueler! Minka is so sensitive. It would absolutely destroy her. Thank heaven she *wasn't* there. She probably went to see Maddie. Or Tommy. I'll call Kate because she knew about Keith's wanting this private talk today. Maybe she picked Minka up to play with the twins."

"Mother, stop. You and I both know that's not possible," Jamie said, feeling her first frisson of fear. "And I can tell the way you said it that you know Kate would never do that without telling me. Neither would Maddie. And Joe would never take Minka to play with Tommy without asking me."

"Oh. Wait a minute, honey," Ellie said. "How about that friend from school with the broken leg she spent so much time with last summer."

"Who? I never heard of any friend with a broken leg, Mom. Where did you get that from?"

"She only mentioned her once in passing and I never heard a name or where she lived. Never mind. It's just all I can think of," Ellie said, her voice now shaky too. "I'll call Kate and Maddie and Joe anyway, Jamie. Just in case they have some ideas about where she might be. I'll call you back."

Recognizing her mother's nervousness scared Jamie even more. Without putting her phone down, Jamie punched Keith's cell number. "You've reached Dr. Keith Summers," his medical voice on the answering machine, "please leave a message. If this is an emergency, please go to the nearest emergency room or call 911."

Just hearing his voice was painful. "Call me as soon as possible Keith. I need to know if Minka is with you."

Suddenly Jamie realized that for the first time in 12 years, she didn't know where her daughter was. It was already getting dark at 6 o'clock. Dark out and her daughter wasn't home. Running to Minka's bedroom, Jamie felt panic like bile in her throat. Minka always made sure her mother knew where she was. A note. Please let there be a note on her bed.

The patchwork quilt with the bright reds and golds on Minka's neatly made bed was one Aunt Nina had bought from Aunt Annie's antique store. But no note. Not under the pillow. Not on her old oak school desk. Jamie stood motionless, breathing in all she could of Minka from this room as if it would help find her. Then she stared at the new University of Michigan poster on the wall.

Jamie had been surprised Minka wanted it for her birthday. She said it was because her grandfather had gone to medical school there and she knew Jamie would have graduated in one more semester. But this still felt odd to Jamie. This new loyalty to the University of Michigan coming out of nowhere.

She started to close the half open closet door when something on the floor in the corner caught her eye. Jamie picked it up and was still staring at a thick blue mitten when her phone rang.

"Jamie," Keith said quickly. "Sorry I missed your call, but I'm on my way back to Chicago and of course Minka isn't with me. You'd know if she was. What's going on?" Angry as she'd been just hours ago, now Jamie felt a stab of affection as she heard the panic in his voice. He loved Minka as much as she did.

"Keith, you knew she was supposed to go to my mother's so you could talk…so we could talk alone." This had to be a 'we,' right now. Not Minka's father against her mother.

"Yes. She told me that on the way home from lunch. And she didn't? Are you telling me she didn't go to Ellie's?"

"No. She didn't. Keith, do you remember her saying she was going to look for a mitten she might have lost on the beach?"

"A blue one. Yes. She showed us the one she still had. I assumed she was going to go look for it and then go to Ellie's."

"So did I. But I was too upset, nervous–whatever about, well what you wanted to talk about. I really wasn't paying attention."

"I wasn't either, Jamie," his clinical tone gone. "For the same reason."

Jamie again felt a flutter of solidarity. The talk about custody had devastated him too. "Keith, I just found the other blue mitten in Minka's closet like she'd thrown it there in a hurry to hide it."

"What are you trying to say, Jamie?"

"Minka didn't go back to the beach because she hadn't lost a mitten."

"I'm still not following you, Jamie."

"Keith. Minka never intended to go to my mother's. You know she's a planner. She figured if I checked in with Mom and she wasn't there, I would just tell Mom she was on the beach looking for her mitten."

"Why? Why not just go where she was supposed to?"

Jamie felt a charging headache strike between her temples. "I don't know but I have a terrible thought, Keith. She knew we were going to talk about her since she couldn't be there. We both know she always wants to know everything, especially now that you're moving away."

"Jamie, what are you saying?"

"Last summer Casey told me he thought Minka had been in the Sandpiper when she was supposed to be on the beach."

"So what?" Keith said.

"We'd just found out you were moving to Tucson so Casey figured maybe she overheard us talk about it. And after that she never did ask us what we thought about your leaving. That just wasn't like her. What if, Keith, what if she did that today? Overheard our whole conversation when we thought she'd left?" Jamie's head felt ready to explode.

"Oh, dear God, Jamie. No, no, no! All the things I said." Jamie could not miss the depth of remorse in his voice.

"And now she's run away," Keith finished. "I'm turning around in a rest stop right now. I'll be back before eleven. And, Jamie, be strong. We'll find her."

'Be strong' meant don't start drinking. Keith knew her disease too well. But she was safe with the Antabuse. For now.

Hurrying up the sloped path, Jamie heard Casey's big voice when she opened the door to the Sandpiper. Just that gave her the first glimmer of hope. Chief of Police Brennan. He would take over and know what to do.

Jamie fell into her mother's open arms as they wept on each other's shoulders. Pete came over and quietly embraced them both. "We'll find her, Jamie," Pete said. "Casey called it in and every patrol car in West Michigan has her description.

"Kate is home in case Minka calls or shows up there. Same with Maddie. Joe is on his way here and we're all going to the beach."

"The beach? Why the beach?" Jamie half sobbed.

"No. Not what you're thinking. It's just so we feel like we're doing something instead of just sitting here. Maybe find somebody walking the beach who's seen her. Pogo's not around so he must be with her. No protection better than that guy."

Jamie felt a flutter of relief. She knew that better than anyone. She could almost hear her attacker screaming as a stray black dog appeared from nowhere, sinking his teeth into the man's arm and driving him off. And that stray dog became Pogo, a cherished member of the Cameron family.

"That's the first good news I've heard, Pete. And Pogo does follow Minka whenever she goes out the door.

"I'm coming to the beach with you." Jamie handed Ellie her cell phone. "In case someone calls, Mom. Why didn't Minka ever ask for a cell phone? Dear God, if she only had one now."

*   *   *

Minka stared at the phone as she finished her second cup of hot chocolate, the fire taking away the chill as the cottage was heating up. Pogo's dinner of stale crackers from the almost empty pantry seemed to have satisfied him as he lay in his usual spot close to the fire.

It was almost six and she still hadn't called the one person she needed to talk to the most right now. Here Andrea was waiting for someone to keep her alive by donating new lungs while Minka was being told she had to choose which parent she wanted to live with when they'd be thousands of miles apart. No. Andrea's and her heartaches didn't compare. And she couldn't pretend they did.

Desperate as she was to talk to Andrea, Minka just couldn't call her. Andrea's generous spirit would take in her best friend's pain. That stress was the last thing Andrea needed right now. No. Minka had left home on her own and she would have to finish this on her own.

Minka was opening a can of soup when her cell phone vibrated in her pocket. Andrea!!! She almost dropped her cell she grabbed it so fast. "Are you getting lungs?" she half yelled.

"Silly goose," Andrea answered with a little chuckle. "Not yet. But if a call from U hospital comes while we're talking," Minka could hear the labored breathing, "I'm hanging up on you. And don't ask me how I knew you weren't going to call me.

"Since the day you and Pogo came to my flute practice like I was the Pied Piper, you and I have had a spiritual connection. We both know it. You were supposed to call me right after you listened in on what your dad wanted to talk about. I gave you time. But when it got to be five here, it was six there and that was it. I know it's bad, so tell me."

In spite of the strained breathing, just hearing Andrea's voice soothed Minka–like the Balm of Gilead in the hymn they both liked.

"Andrea, I came here on my bike without telling anyone. I didn't mean to bring Pogo–but he just showed up and came too. And I'm glad," she said as Pogo lifted his head at hearing his name. "Andrea, I needed to talk to you more than anyone in the world. But I, I just wasn't going to call you. And you know why."

"I'd like to say 'duh,' Minka, but that's rude. If it had gone well, you'd have called me right away. But because whatever you heard was bad, you didn't call. I'm facing a double lung transplant and you didn't want to give me more stress."

"'There you go again, my best friend in the world. Saying out loud the very words I'm thinking. And 'duh' yourself! You wouldn't have called either if you were in my place. As for the Pied Piper, Pogo and I do not happen to be rats."

Andrea's familiar giggle came in Minka's ear and she found herself laughing with tears running down her face. "How can you make me laugh, Andrea? All I want to do is sob and feel sorry for myself while you're the one who has the right to feel sorry for yourself!"

"Your laugh just made my day! And if I don't get a lung donor call pretty soon, I will feel sorry for myself. Right now before you tell me what you heard today, we need to talk business. Does anyone know where you are?"

"Yes. You and Pogo."

"That's your obnoxious way of saying 'no.' So here's the deal. I don't care what went on between your mother and father today, they do not deserve to worry about where you are. Nor do Elliegram and Casey and Maddie and Kate and Tommy or anyone who loves you."

"But..." Minka started.

"No buts. You're my mature, smart 12-year-old who skipped a grade, remember? Don't act like a whiny adolescent now. When we hang up, you're going to pick one of them to call who will assure your family that you're safe and in no danger. You don't need to tell them any more than that.

"And you can stay where you are until you're ready to go home–whenever. Are we clear on this? By the way, I'll ask Bruce to drop off some food for you tomorrow. And he's CIA trustworthy."

"Pretty bossy," Minka said knowing Andrea was right. "I would have gotten around to calling later tonight. But, now, okay. I'll call when we hang up."

"So I'm hanging up now..." Andrea started to say when Minka interrupted her. "Wait. I have one thing to tell you. I found my literature book from Mrs. Fowler's class and hadn't written any notes by your poem, but I did memorize it. 'My little horse must think it queer...'"

"To stop without a farmhouse near," Andrea finished.

"Oh, Minka. How I miss our reading times together. Perseus and Icarus and the Minotaur. At least we can still talk about our books. And I have to concede Maddie is right about **The Hunger Games**. It was the pageturner I needed right now. And I just started **Catching Fire**."

"I'd like to say 'I told you so,' but you'd call me immature so I won't. But guess what book I brought here in my backpack? **The Mockingjay**."

"I would have called you immature, M. Save this new book for me–maybe I'll be reading it with new lungs! But now you need to hang up. Your family's worried to death...Oops, another Freudian slip by me...worried sick about you. Call whomever you want. But I'm hanging up and you're calling. Then call me right back and tell me what happened today that made you run away."

Andrea clicked off before Minka could say goodbye. Again, Andrea had said what Minka knew, but needed her best friend to put it into words. She was being a whiny child punishing her parents by scaring them. She dialed the cell number she knew by heart.

"Don't say a word and go where no one can hear you right now, Tommy."

"Min…" he stopped. "Hey, Billy," he spoke out clearly. "How you doing?" Minka heard Tommy walking and then a door closing.

"Where in hell are you?" Tommy asked in a stifled voice. "Everyone in town is looking for you. Why do you keep doing such dumb stuff, Minka! You would have scared me if I didn't know you so well. You're a cat with seven lives."

"Nine, not seven, Tommy. Now listen to me please."

"Both ears."

"What if Aunt Brenda and Uncle Joe were getting divorced and your dad was moving to the other side of the country for good and you had to choose which one you wanted to live with?"

Minka knew Brenda and Joe O'Connor adopted Tommy when his parents died in a car accident. They could never have their own children and Tommy was Joe's nephew. So when Tommy's parents were killed, Joe and Brenda adopted him. Minka knew no child loved his biological parents more than Tommy loved his uncle and aunt.

Tommy didn't answer right away. "That sucks, Minka." Another pause. "I would run away too."

"I knew you'd get it, Tommy. That's why you're the only person I'm calling. I need your help."

"Name it."

"I need you to call your dad as a reporter who can't reveal his sources–especially if it's his son–to tell my parents I'm safe and will talk to them when I'm ready. And that Pogo is with me."

"I'll call him as soon as we hang up, Minka. I didn't know you had a cell phone. "

"It's a long story. You can call me on this number, but I don't want anyone else to have it yet. Not even your dad."

"You got it. And wherever you are, I'm just so damn glad you're okay. I knew you would be, but, well, it's good to hear your voice, Minka."

"That's your second cuss word tonight, Tommy."

"And I'm saving some of my really good ones if you don't take care of yourself!"

"Hey. I'm cool. I have your rabbit's foot in my hand right now."

"So it's nine lives, not seven. Later."

Minka rubbed the furry charm against her cheek as she patted Pogo with her other hand. Tommy was 14 now and had always been like a big brother to her. She thought about what Mr. Armitage had said to her about being Andrea's little sister. She decided God had a special heart for only children. So He had found a brother and sister for her, and a sister for both Andrea and Tommy!

Promises To Keep

DAWN SATURDAY NOVEMBER 27, 2010

It was still dark out when Minka checked her phone. 5:23 a.m. She still wasn't used to having a cell phone, but already counted on it. She clicked the answering ring on along with vibrate because she didn't need to hide it anymore. Pogo was the only one who could hear it. "And you won't tell anyone I have a phone, will you, Pogo Boy."

She stretched out in the chair she'd slept in, comforted by the warmth of the fire she'd left on. She couldn't bring herself to sleep in Andrea's room—too much of Andrea there. And she didn't want to dirty any sheets in one of the other bedrooms. As she puffed up the throw pillow she'd slept with, Minka knew she could last a long time sleeping nights on this leather chair.

"I know it's early to get up," she scratched Pogo's ears. "But you need to do your business while it's still dark out so no one sees us." Minka had defrosted a package of ground beef the night before wondering if Andrea had her mother leave it in the freezer on purpose. It wouldn't surprise her. Sometimes Andrea was like one of the Oracles who could see what was going to happen before it did.

"I bet you won't mind eating early," Minka said to the dog attentively watching as she chopped up some hamburger with more crackers in a soup bowl from the cupboard. She filled another bowl with water and put both down for Pogo. She smiled at his tail wagging in high speed at this luxury breakfast while she ate the protein bar she'd grabbed before leaving the log cabin.

She turned on her flashlight and shut off the lights, even though they couldn't be seen from the road. Tommy had said everyone was looking for her.

But she hoped they'd stopped once Uncle Joe told them she was safe and asked them not to try and find her. She knew Casey would call off the police search.

Minka put on her coat, boots, earmuffs, and gloves, wishing she'd thought of a better lie than the thermal blue mittens. She'd really like to have them right now. But cold as the air felt while they headed out the door to the beach, Minka knew it would be worse without the lake effect. Lake Michigan's water was warmer than the land keeping the air temperature higher than it would have been otherwise.

"Thank you again, Big Lake," she said as she followed the flashlight beam down the stairs to the beach, Pogo already running ahead in the sand.

Half an hour later, Pogo had been wiped down in the garage, and Minka was getting ready to shower in the guest bathroom when her cell rang. "Did they call? Tell me they did?" she yelled into the phone.

"Hey. It's me," Tommy said. "I don't know about any call but I'm just letting you know everyone is cool at your house. Maybe not 'cool,' but relieved to know you're safe. Dad said they all did their best to find out who had called him–especially Chief Brennan. But they had no chance against Dad's 'confidential source'."

"Did Uncle Joe ask why I called you?"

"Nada, Minka. He knows you called me because we've been best friends since you learned to walk. Dad knows we've always trusted each other. He'd never interfere with that."

"If it weren't for your dad, I never would have found mine," she said. Then she thought about what Andrea had said. "And if I hadn't met him, I wouldn't be so sad that he's moving. But I also wouldn't have a dad. Uncle Joe did that for me, Tommy."

"And Gloria, remember? It's my favorite family story. I'll keep you posted on the home front and you call me any time. Hang in there, Minka."

"I've got my good luck furry foot!"

Minka stayed in the shower longer than usual, the pounding hot water stinging her skin helping to focus her mind. She was a planner but this had happened so fast, she had no idea what she was going to do now. She'd felt torn between her parents since summer, but neither of them knew it. Only Andrea did.

But now? Now was she going to be forced to choose? Which parent she liked better? Andrea had talked about King Solomon offering to solve the same problem by cutting the baby in two. Tears began mixing with the shower water. That's just what it felt like. Being cut in two.

She was zipping up her jeans when the phone rang. Why would Tommy call again so soon…she grabbed the phone with both hands and didn't finish her 'hello.'

"The transplant nurse called! They have lungs for me!" Minka fell to her knees on the hard tile and could only mumble words of joy and prayer between sobs. "And I'm the only one they're calling, M."

"What do you mean," Minka exclaimed as she stood up. "Only'?"

"Oh, no. M, sometimes they bring in two patients for the same organ donation and test them to see which one is more likely to…well, you know, make it. I'm sorry, but I didn't tell you because…."

"Because I would have worried even more–and I would have! I'm grateful I didn't know that, Andrea. God bless you for knowing me so well."

"M, please come," Andrea said as she took a deep breath. "My donor is from Wisconsin so the lungs will arrive in Ann Arbor within hours. Please say you'll come, M."

"I promise," Minka said. She had always planned on her mom or dad taking her to Ann Arbor when the call came that Andrea had donor lungs. That's when she would finally tell them about who Andrea was. But now? Which one to ask? King Solomon again.

"Now we both have promises to keep," Andrea said.

"Yes, we do, Andrea. Maddie will bring me," Minka said suddenly! Of course Maddie would.

"Dad will call you with details, my dear M. Oh, I'm just so discombobulated. I even asked if they were sure the lungs were for me? Some lung transplant patients wait a year for a donor and it's not even four months for me. I was afraid they'd made a mistake, M. And then the nurse said they were for me if I would accept them!!! Accept them?"

Suddenly Andrea broke into her familiar giggle sending Minka into hysterics. They were both crying and laughing together until Andrea had a coughing spell. "See you," she managed to say before she hung up.

Maddie picked up on the second ring. "Maddie, it's me and don't say my name if someone's with you."

"Dear God in heaven, I'm so happy to hear your voice, Minka. And, no. I'm driving home from visiting Ben at Recovery Strong where he's been in rehab since he left detox."

"He better not leave early like my mom did. Maddie, I have a really huge favor to ask. I mean really huge."

"You rapscallion, you! We were all so hysterically happy when Joe told us last night you were safe there's probably nothing I wouldn't do for you right now. Name it."

Minka inhaled as she went into her fast talk. Hardly taking a breath, Minka began with the flute music and how Pogo thought it was Maddie playing, summarizing until she got to today's transplant donor's call. "And I promised Andrea I'd be there for her surgery today."

"Double lungs?" Maddie said in disbelief. "I didn't know they could..., well, of course I'll take you. She's your dearest friend facing, well, well, she needs you. Ann Arbor's almost three hours away. I know where U Hospital is and I'll get you there before two. I just need to get a hold of Gail and tell her to take over Monday for a few days and then run home and pack for an overnight. Maybe more. Do you need me to get clothes from your house?"

"I brought enough in my backpack with me yesterday. And I'm not ready for either of my parents yet. They don't know about Andrea and I don't want to tell them now. We can drop Pogo off with Tommy on our way out of town. I'll text you the directions to where the Armitage cottage is. That's where I am."

"I'm on my way, sweetheart."

"Oh, Maddie." Suddenly Minka felt like a lost little girl, not a tough twelve-year-old. "I love you."

"Oh, honey. You have no idea how much I love you."

*   *   *

"How can you not have a picture of Andrea?" Maddie looked over at her front-seat passenger. "You've been talking about her since we left and we're almost in Ann Arbor, Minka. I feel like I know her already—and now I love her a little bit too. What a remarkable young woman she must be to have so much compassion for you while she's dealing with an incurable illness! And struggling just to breathe. I want to know what she looks like."

Minka thought about the almost translucent glow she'd seen on Andrea's face from the day they'd met. "It's hard to describe her. Don't laugh but she reminded me of an angel the first time I saw her."

"Actually, I'm not even all that surprised," Maddie said passing a black truck. "Six years older and she spent her summer as your special friend. And I now know you really needed one. And I also understand why you couldn't talk to me about it. I'm too close to your mom, and you didn't want her to know your dad was pushing you to move away with him.

"Plus the water spitting! Laboring to breathe sure hasn't hurt Andrea's sense of humor. And then all the literature you guys read together. I wish it weren't in a hospital, Minka, but I honestly can't wait to meet her. Angel might be the best description of…hey, your cell phone's ringing."

"Sorry, I thought it was yours. I'm not used to having one," Minka said pulling it out of her jacket pocket.

"Hello, Nana," she spoke into the cell. "Oh, me too. Not even a half hour now. That's very kind. Her name is Maddie Langston. Yes. We'll do that. And you too, Nana.

"That was Andrea's grandmother Nana who's riding with Andrea's mother from Chicago so they'll have a car in Ann Arbor. She called to say they have a reservation for us at the Ronald McDonald House. But Andrea and her dad are already in admissions so she said we should go straight to the University Hospital and ask for the transplant floor."

Suddenly Minka felt tears coming and squeezed the rabbit foot with both hands. "Oh, now I'm scared, Maddie. This is too real. Andrea's going to have her chest cut…"

"Stop! Stop," Maddie put her hand on Minka's leg. "We're not dealing with that yet. First we have to clear the air between us. Then Andrea gets our full attention. I know your mom and dad had an ugly fight yesterday and your mom thinks that's why you took off. The first question you have to tell me honestly is if you knew what they were fighting about. The second, if so, how did you find out?"

Minka stared silently out the car window letting the tears roll down her face.

"Minka, I know this feels like piling on right now. You're so worried about Andrea and now your parents. But I want to help you just like you're wanting to help Andrea. But I can't if I don't know why you ran away."

Without moving her head, Minka wiped her arm across her wet face and said quietly, "My parents want me to choose between living in Arizona with my dad or Spring Port with my mother. If I don't choose, the courts will decide."

"OH shit!" Maddie said loudly. "Sorry. Sorry. Oh, dearest Minka. Your mom told all of us that your dad now wants custody. I don't need to tell you how infuriated we were. And still are. But nothing about..I mean never

100

that YOU should choose!! Oh, my God, Minka. I can't imagine! My dad was my best friend, but my mother needed me to take care of her. If I'd had to choose…." Maddie shook her head. Then she grabbed Minka's hand and kissed it.

Minka watched the snowflakes swirl outside her window. "I've listened in all summer," Minka finally said looking over at Maddie. "Ever since my dad said he was moving. Andrea was the only person who knew I was eavesdropping. I told her everything because she was so, so accepting, so understanding–as if she'd already known. And she never said an unkind word about either my dad or mom. We told each other everything. What I couldn't talk to mom about and what she couldn't talk to her parents about.

"Nobody said anything in front of me about my dad's moving away, but I knew they talked about it when I wasn't around. It was easy to listen in at the Sandpiper. But at our cabin I had to make a hiding place in the hall closet. I needed to know why my dad had to talk to my mom alone after he and I had lunch. So I pretended to leave and hid in the closet where I could hear them talk. That's how I found out about the plan to make me choose."

Then she pointed out the windshield, "Look, Maddie. There's the sign to U Hospital's parking garage." Minka leaned back in her seat, grateful to have the conversation over.

"Thank you, Minka, for telling me all of it. And I can promise you one thing," Maddie said turning into the garage. "You are not going to choose. I promise you that. So now that's out of the way, you can be all about Andrea. And I can't wait to meet her. Let's go."

{ 18 }

Promises To Keep

1P.M. SATURDAY, NOVEMBER 27, 2010

A pretty a dark-haired woman wearing a white medical coat with University of Michigan embroidered on it greeted them. "I'm Lisa and I'll show you where to hang your coats. Cool top," she said to Minka about her navy shirt with the big gold M on the front. "I think Andrea had one on just like it when she came in today."

Minka grinned, "She better have!"

"Well, you must be her special friend Minka. She's asked more than once if you were here yet so I've been on the lookout. My name is Lisa Farr, and I'll be Andrea's P.A. for the surgery."

Looking at Minka with a huge smile of perfect white teeth, Lisa said, "And since you don't look quite old enough to drive yet," she looked at Maddie, "you must be the nice friend who drove Minka here on very short notice."

"Yes. I'm Maddie Langston. And for several reasons," she raised her eyebrows at Minka, "I was very glad to get the call from her this morning that she needed a ride." Lisa held out a bottle of hand sanitizers from the nursing station counter for both of them to use. "And I've never met Andrea, so I look forward to it. This one," she gestured toward Minka, "talked about her pretty much all the way here."

"I'm not surprised," Lisa said leading them down a long corridor toward the elevator. "Andrea's now entertaining all of us in the transplant unit." Then she paused and looked at them. "But before then she did have a little meltdown going through admissions with her dad. She kept asking me and everyone around who the donor was and what could she do for the family, getting more and more upset. Fortunately that's when Dr. Rasmussen came by to introduce himself as her surgeon.

"Dr. Rasmussen has been through this before. Very quietly–he is a gentle soul–but firmly, he told her she had to put those questions aside for now. The best thing she could do for the donor family was to calm down and stay upbeat for her operation. And then she could thank the family by having a great life with her donor's lungs.

"It was like a light bulb going on, I swear," Lisa said as she led them into the elevator and punched the button to the transplant floor. "Andrea just sat in her wheelchair for a minute. Then she looks right at Dr. Rasmussen and says, 'Does your wife know I'm sleeping with you tonight?'"

Minka started laughing. "Of course she did. I can pretty much hear her. And I'm not surprised by what happened while she was being admitted. She was so grateful to get on the donor list, but as soon as she did, she started agonizing that someone had died for her to get the lungs."

"Andrea is the smartest person I've ever known, Lisa. Once her doctor told her what she had to do, she was done with the donor sadness until the surgery's over. Then her goofy side took over. It's so Andrea."

"She must be a great friend to have," Lisa said as the elevator doors opened to the Transplant Center. "Here she looks like Miss Innocence with those huge blue eyes as she gets her blood drawn. And then she tells everyone in the room about her date with Dr. Rasmussen tonight."

"Now I really can't wait to meet Andrea," Maddie said as they followed Lisa down the highly polished floor. A loudspeaker broke the quiet seriousness in the place where failing body organs get removed and replaced with healthy ones. "Dr. Puri," the loudspeaker sounded. "Call from four G for Dr. Baer."

A nurse in navy scrubs with a gold block M on the front walked past them wheeling a medical device on its own steel dolly. "A portable X-Ray machine," Lisa said. "We use that a lot on this floor."

Lisa had barely opened the door before Andrea saw them. "It's about time," she called out as Lisa led Minka and Maddie into a treatment room where Andrea was seated in a reclining brown chair.

"Look at you!" she said pointing at Minka's navy top with the big gold 'M'. I had mine on until they put me in this hospital gown so they could stick this needle in my arm."

Andrea was hooked up to a clear bag hanging on a stand filled with blood. "I'll squeeze harder now that you're here," Andrea held out the rubber pump in her hand. "Dad went to make phone calls when Lisa told him you were here.

"Hi, Maddie. I'm Andrea and I know you're M's great friend and driver. I'd give you a thank you hug, Maddie, but," she raised her arms a little, "I'm pretty tied up. And I can't tell you how grateful I am for getting M here–my new name for her since she put on that shirt," Andrea pointed at it.

"I knew she didn't want to ask one of her parents to drive her. That would be like choosing and she's not doing that. I promised her that wasn't going to happen." She looked directly at Minka. "Just one of the promises I will keep."

Minka blew Andrea an air kiss as Maddie said, "I'm with you on that, Andrea. We won't let it happen. And I'm so glad to meet you, even though I feel like I know you after all Mink...M has told me about you."

"Well, I don't dare ask what, Maddie, but M knows me better than anyone else. And now I'm going to have Dad get you a Michigan shirt like ours because that big M stands for your name too! Come sit down by me," Andrea pointed to some molded plastic chairs.

"But why do they need so much blood?" Minka asked Lisa as she and Maddie sat down. "I'd think she'd need it all for her operation."

Andrea did her endearing giggle. "Lisa, my young friend here," she gestured with her free hand, "is the queen of questions."

"But a logical one," Lisa said. "They need all that blood before they operate, M, to check for any infection and make sure Andrea has a stable blood count. They check her electrolytes, kidney and liver to make sure they're all normal."

The curly blond haired nurse taking the blood slowly removed the needle, putting a cotton ball inside Andrea's elbow, and bending it up. "Finally done," she said, "and try and keep your arm up to keep pressure on to prevent any bleeding. You did a good job, Andrea."

"And now I need to take her to the shower," Lisa said helping Andrea into a wheel chair.

"My second of the day because I took one at home," Andrea said, her arm still in the air.

"But for this one you need a full antiseptic body scrub," Lisa explained.

"Is this before or after my enema?" Andrea asked smiling at all of them.

"I told you she's making trouble," Lisa said wheeling Andrea out of the room. "You two can wait in her room in the holding unit. Someone at the nursing station will show you which one it is. And just down the hall there's a little break room with coffee and tea and snacks. But you'll have time to go to the cafeteria if you haven't had lunch."

"You both should eat," Andrea said over her shoulder, "because I'm kind of like Frost, Minka. I have "hours and hours" before my date with Dr. Rasmussen."

Lisa turned around, "See what I told you?"

Ignoring the levity, Minka called after them in a deeply serious voice, "And you have promises to keep too, Andrea. You can't forget." Andrea gave a V for victory sign over her head as the wheelchair vanished around the corner.

Minka and Maddie sat quietly beside the empty hospital bed in the holding area, full-length blue curtains around the space separating the cubicle from the empty beds on both sides. Pointing at the complex of electronic monitors on the wall behind the bed, Minka finally said, "I can't help but think about all the patients who have been in this bed before. Waiting for new kidneys. Or a liver or a heart. But Andrea's surgery will be harder than theirs was and her risk of rejection..."

"Hey stop," Maddie interrupted her just as her cell phone beeped. "You need to get your happy back right now. And this is your mom texting. She wants me to call her if I've heard anything more about where you are." Maddie looked hard at Minka. "I know how stressed she is. And she is my best friend."

Minka thought about how her mom had taken Maddie in as a neglected teenager. That was how she knew Maddie would drop everything today to drive her. "Is it okay if I'm not ready to talk to her? Or my dad?"

"Of course it is. And you can hear everything I tell her," Maddie elbowed Minka's arm, "without being in a closet." Then she pulled on Minka's thick dark ponytail and dialed. "Hey Jamie, Minka's fine, we're in Ann Arbor–it's a long story and I don't have time now for the details. But here's the short version."

Minka was actually relieved as she heard Maddie tell about the eavesdropping, running away rather than having to choose. About her private friendship with Andrea. Explaining they were now at the University of Michigan Hospital for a double lung transplant took a little longer.

"Jamie, Andrea's coming into this pre-op holding area any minute so I have to go. Yes, the surgery is today. Soon. Yes, of course I'll tell her." Minka tapped her arm and mouthed, "Tell Mom I love her."

"And she says the same to you...oh, here's Andrea now. Love."

"Hey guys. I'm so glad to see you both here. Especially as this is my last stop before Dr. Rasmussen," Andrea said as an orderly and Lisa pushed her wheelchair forward and lifted her onto the bed.

"And," Andrea looked at Minka and Maddie, "my dad said to thank you both for being her because he's in the waiting room on another floor with my mom. She's getting a headache and they're worried about germs. Even though I'm pretty sure no germ has a chance with me I'm scrubbed so clean my skin's going to slough. Have you guys eaten?"

"When you go to the O.R., we will," Minka said. "And you'll be happy to know Maddie just told my mom all about you so now I don't have to."

"Even the closet part?" Andrea asked with a half grin.

"That too," Maddie was saying just as Andrea put her finger over her lips.

"Hear that?" Andrea asked as an engine sounded overhead.

"That's the helicopter carrying my new lungs packed in a cooler filled with ice." Andrea looked up, her hands folded together in prayer. "His name was Levi and he was 31 and overdosed last night on heroin. His family told Dr. Rasmussen they wanted me to know before surgery. They thought it would help me do well for his sake. And they want to meet me when I'm able to and they're ready."

"It's very unusual for the donor family to share this so soon," Lisa said as she straightened the blanket over Andrea. "But his mother is an intensive care nurse and the whole family is registered with Gift of Life. They wanted Andrea and everyone else to know hoping their son's organ donations could encourage others to sign up."

Lisa shook her head as she said, "The only good outcome of this opioid epidemic is that these are usually younger, healthier people whose organs are donated. Enough talk about that. Just ring that buzzer if you need anything, Andrea. That helicopter means it won't be long now.

"And you two keep her entertained. I'll be right down at the nursing station."

"Hey, before you leave," Andrea said. "What you told me about my donor's parents wanting me to know about their son? That really does help. Like he and I are kind of a team–a relay team. He hands off to me what I can't live without. I hate it that he died, but, now–in a way he didn't. Did they donate all his organs?"

"Now who's the Queen of Questions? Yes and no more donor questions."

As Lisa closed the curtain behind her, Minka put her hand on Andrea's foot under the covers. "So remember what you said the day your dad gave me this," she held up the iPhone, "and you gave me this," she pointed at her shirt.

"Yes," Andrea nodded. "And you complained about too many presents."

"And," Minka went on, "you said you loved gifts. So it's my turn." She handed Andrea a small tissue wrapped package.

"It sounds like expensive jewelry," Andrea said about the small clicking sound as she opened it. Then her eyes lit up as she pulled out a well worn rabbit's foot on a key chain. Nobody spoke as Andrea began rubbing the white fur against her cheek.

{ 1 9 }

P r o m i s e s   T o   K e e p

8P.M. SATURDAY, NOVEMBER 27, 2010

Minka had held it together blowing safe kisses as they wheeled Andrea out of the blue-curtained holding room to surgery. The last few minutes before she left had been busy with the doctor and residents and Lisa coming in with last minute checks and instructions. But watching Mr. Armitage walk beside Andrea's rolling bed toward the operating room had been too much. Maddie had pulled her into her arms, letting Minka's sobs rock her too. With her own face streaming tears, Maddie had said, "Good for you not to break down in front of Andrea."

Now they were settled with Andrea's dad in the private waiting room for transplant families staring blankly at CNN trying not to look at the clock. Andrea had been in the O.R. almost two hours, and they were nervously waiting for the circulating nurse to call Andrea's dad with updates.

Brad Armitage had insisted Andrea's mother and grandmother wait in their room at the Ronald McDonald House because neither of them felt well. None of them said it, but all three knew that with Nana's age and Barbara Armitage's anxiety, the stress of waiting in the hospital was too much for both of them. Brad promised to call them the minute he heard from the O.R.

"I see where Andrea's beautiful blue eyes came from," Maddie said to Brad Armitage trying to make conversation.

"Yes, but her skill with horses came from her mother," he replied.

"I'd love to hear about that, Mr. Armitage," Minka said. "I saw her picture with the trophy. She told me she liked stadium jumping the best."

He broke out in a smile. "Oh she did and she was a fearless competitor." Then his voice flattened. "We're counting on her using that courage right now…"

They all turned toward the sound of footsteps. A broad-shouldered man in navy scrubs with a surgery mask hanging around his neck and a clipboard in his hand came in.

"Hello, folks, I'm Dr. Steve Slater, one of Dr. Rasmussen's thoracic residents taking care of Andrea. He asked me to come by and see if you had any questions I could answer. And I want to make sure you're doing okay. Before you ask, no, I don't have an update, but soon. Judy, the circulating nurse, will call you, Brad, on that phone," he pointed at the wall phone.

"Thank you for coming in, Dr. Slater," Mr. Armitage said, "and these are Andrea's friends. Minka Cameron in the Michigan shirt and her friend Maddie Langston who drove here this morning from Spring Port on Lake Michigan."

Mr. Armitage had barely finished when Minka said, "I do have one question, Dr. Slater. Why do people who get lung transplants have more rejections than people who get a heart or kidneys or other organs?"

"You must be M because before she went to sleep Andrea said her friend M would be the one to ask all the questions. The answer is simple." He opened his mouth wide, then inhaled a big breath through his nose. "If there were any germs in the air," he motioned around him, "they'd go straight through my nose and mouth into my lungs exposing them to infection. A transplanted heart or kidneys or liver–they're all insulated inside the body away from airborne germs.

"I brought some drawings of the surgery if you want to see them. Not everyone does." He looked around. "I thought you would," he said as all three moved toward him.

He pulled a laminated artist's colored rendering of a torso from his clipboard. "This," he pointed to a black marker line running from under the right arm, across the chest under the breasts and into the left underarm side of the torso, "is one of the biggest incisions anyone ever has to have." He showed where the sternum has to be broken and opened like a clamshell to get to the lungs.

"I know this is a lot to…" The phone rang. Dr. Slater started to reach for it, then stopped. "Sorry. My conditioned response when the phone rings. It will be for you from the operating room, Mr. Armitage."

Paul held up his palm and said, "Please. Since you're here could you?"

Nodding knowingly, he answered, "It's Dr. Slater for Andrea's dad. Hey, Judy." As he listened quietly, he made the okay sign with his fingers and the sighs of relief were audible. He listened for a minute, then thanked her. "I'll tell them.

"So far, so good. The first lung is out and we remove the worst one first. Judy said it was so scarred they don't know how Andrea got any oxygen through it. She said Andrea's skin color is already pinker now that she has one good lung to breathe with."

Brad Armitage had his arms around Maddie's and Minka's shoulders, his bright blue eyes shiny wet, both girls leaning into him with their own tears.

Dr. Slater looked at his watch. "That first lung started at 5:15 p.m. and it's just after 8 so that's about three hours, about what Dr. Rasmussen expected. Now he and his team will be taking a break, bathroom and stretching and probably some food and coffee.

"So," he checked his watch again, "it's going to be after 11 tonight before they're all done. One of the orderlies is bringing you some blankets and pillows. These chairs fold back almost like a bed. Turn the lights down and try to sleep. You still have a long night ahead."

Two hours later, Andrea's P.A. Lisa walked Jamie and Ellie to the transplant waiting room. When they got there, the room was so silent they hesitated to open the door. "Trust me, they're all in there," Lisa whispered. "But I doubt they're sleeping. In any case they'll want to see you."

Jamie quietly peeked into the dimly lit room when she heard the voice she'd desperately missed. "Mom, I can see you!" Suddenly Jamie was holding her daughter with both arms tight enough to keep her from ever running away again. Then Ellie embraced them both as the lights went on.

"You're here!" Maddie called from the corner, climbing out of the reclining chair. "I'm so glad to see you two."

"Well, same here," Jamie said as she and Ellie gave her a quick hug.

"This is Minka's mother Jamie Cameron and her grandmother Ellie Brennan," Maddie said to the tall man in a rumpled sports coat walking toward them with his hand reaching out to greet them.

"I'm Brad Armitage, Andrea's father. I can't begin to tell you what a blessing Minka has been to our family. And how grateful I am to Maddie for bringing her here today on such short notice."

For the next few minutes they caught up, Brad explaining the surgery was half done and going well, and why Andrea's mother and grandmother were waiting at the Ronald McDonald House. Ellie said her husband Casey had refused to let the two women drive alone this late when they were both still tired from the night before, and now he was downstairs in the main waiting room.

"Casey didn't think any more people were needed up on the transplant floor," Ellie said.

"Did he have his police light on the car?" Minka asked feeling guilty because she was the reason her mother and grandmother were so tired.

"He did," Ellie said, "so if he drove a little too fast, he wouldn't get pulled over. He knew your mom wanted to see you as soon as possible, Minka."

Suddenly Jamie kneeled in front of her daughter as she grabbed both her hands. "Minka, I can't wait another second to tell you. Your dad's not moving. It's all over. The choosing. Custody. It's done."

Leaning backwards as if away from the words she'd just heard, Minka said blankly, "I don't understand, Mom." Maddie whispered to Brad that she would explain this later.

"Minka," Jamie went on, "you should not have run away, but…well, your dad was so shaken and scared when we didn't know where you were. He really hadn't understood what pain he'd caused you. But it was because he didn't want to live without you."

Minka was paralyzed. On emotional overload. Her heart had been with Andrea since the call this morning and now knowing her chest was carved wide open right now? How could she abandon Andrea's in crisis to take in this miraculous news about herself?

"Oh, baby," Jamie put her hands on Minka's shoulders. "This is too much now. I just couldn't wait to tell you. Your dad is going to be in your life more than ever. It's all in the letter he wrote for you. It's in my purse. Tucson knows he's not taking the job, Pat cancelled their offer on the house there, and he's checking into teaching positions at Michigan State Medical School. They're going to live in Grand Rapids, and you'll be able to see each other all the time. He and Pat can come to your school events."

Minka fell forward into her mother's arms, leaning against Jamie as if she was afraid she might fall. Then she hugged her mother with all the strength she had left in her exhausted body.

"Congratulations, my dear Minka," Brad came over and gently tugged her pony tail. "Maddie just told me what this means to you. It's wonderful news that you deserve," Brad said, his whole face smiling. "And my mother always says good things come in threes. We have one working lung, your dad isn't moving, so now let's pray the third is another good lung."

In what Brad would forever tell his friends was a God moment, the phone rang. This time he grabbed it and almost immediately did a full fist pump into the air as the room broke out in tears and hugs and noisy cheers that filled the room. Suddenly from outside the door, the noise quietly echoed into the room by the sound of discreet clapping coming from the nursing station.

An hour later, Minka was struggling to fall asleep in their room at the Ronald McDonald House when her cell rang. Her heart skipped when she saw it was from Brad Armitage. She stared at the phone half not wanting to pick it up. "Hello," she said swallowing hard.

"I didn't want to wake you up, but Andrea made it known I had to. We both know when she is determined for something to happen, it does!"

Minka's brain flashed on the Scorpio signs, wondering if he knew about them.

"You know she can't talk because of the breathing tube and she's sedated so communicating is a huge strain. But she could hear me and somehow managed to scribble to me what looked like a heart and an OK on a note pad in the five minutes I was allowed in the transplant ICU.

"But as I was leaving she tapped with the pen to stop me and scrawled a big M. I knew it was for you as she scratched out letters I couldn't read. But when she persisted in tapping the M, I knew she meant I had to call you."

Minka was sitting upright in bed and Maddie was now wide awake too.

"I have the paper. I'm looking at it now. Trying to read it but it's really illegible. If I see anything, it's like maybe the letter 'k'. And maybe an 'e' and then a pretty clear 'p.' Yes. It looks like maybe the word 'Keep.'"

{ 2 0 }

Promises To Keep

MOONDAY, DECEMBER 20, 2010

"Well look at you," Minka said as she walked into the lobby at the University of Michigan's transplant aftercare facility to see Andrea walking fast toward her. "I'll race you down the hall," Andrea said.

"Oh no you won't," a stocky nurse with severely cut short grey hair beside her said.

"This is Lady Macbeth," Andrea gestured at the nurse. "Ignore her nametag that says 'Agnes.' And she's thrilled I'm leaving today."

"We might finally have some peace and quiet around here," the nurse said her eyes twinkling behind her wire-framed glasses.

With a big smile, Minka said, "I'm Minka Cameron. And this is Maddie Langston. And we know she can be a trouble maker, Agnes, NOT Lady Macbeth."

"Well, in addition to having already broken every rule here, last week I caught her starting to make a snowman when patients aren't allowed to go outside at all. Let alone by themselves."

"Well one of the interns finished it after I was so rudely interrupted," Andrea said, "and now Frosty's even got a pipe."

Minka stared at her friend. She had never heard Andrea speak in such a strong voice before. No more pauses to breathe, no more deep inhales of breath as she talked. Minka felt her heart flood with pure joy.

"What can I say?" Agnes said throwing up her hands. "I've got you three set up in this conference room," she opened the door to a room and pointed at a round table with chairs around it. "You see the carafe of coffee and homemade cookies from one of our volunteers. Plus the water bottles. And you can see your friend's creation from here."

Minka and Maddie couldn't help laughing when they saw the sloppy little snowman out the window. "Thank you Agnes," Maddie said. "I hope the intern who finished it for Andrea isn't going into plastic surgery."

Agnes tried to stifle a laugh as she pulled out chairs for them. "And of course poor little Frosty's got a Michigan baseball hat on when he's supposed to wear a black stovepipe," Andrea added as they all sat down.

"I have to tell you Andrea," Minka said passing the plate of cookies and opening a water bottle, "when I first met you I was fascinated by your skin because it was so pale it felt like I could see through it. Now it looks like you're wearing makeup."

"The cosmetic is called 'Oxygen,' oops, here comes my doctor."

A grey-haired man in a white coat with a stethoscope around his neck came in, an easy smile on his face. "I'm Dr. Korbuly," he said with a hint of a European accent. "We met when you visited Andrea before she left the hospital. She's feisty, as all of you already know.

"However," he glanced cautiously at Agnes, "not everyone agrees with me. But I'm convinced that spunk is a big reason why she's leaving as our star double lung transplant patient. I probably shouldn't be quoted saying that," this time he looked directly at Agnes, "because it's certainly not in any of our transplant protocols." Then he grinned broadly as Agnes made the zip signal over her lips.

"So now I understand you two have plans to visit Andrea in Chicago over the next few months which will be good for her. She's going to be strictly monitored there at Northwestern Hospital for any signs of rejection and then back here for regular follow-ups as well."

"Don't even ask Dr. Korbuly how many anti-rejection pills I have to take every day," Andrea added.

"And you always will need to," he said.

"Don't remind me! But the good news is that my parents did buy the cottage on Lake Michigan so I'll get to see these guys all summer."

"Can't think of a better place to heal than that, Andrea," Dr. Korbuly said. "Oh, and someone from Gift of Life called Dr. Rasmussen about interviewing you. You're kind of a celebrity in the transplant world now because you're young to have had a double lung transplant. Plus your donor was an opioid addict. Because this opioid epidemic is starting to make regular headlines, getting new lungs from someone who overdosed is newsworthy."

"I can't hold back any longer," Maddie said, "now that you brought it up Dr. Korbuly."

He turned toward her.

"I brought these for Andrea," Maddie pulled a stack of papers out of her purse, "but now I think I should give them to you, Dr. Korbuly.

"My friend, boyfriend—whatever, Ben was an all state athlete in high school who had a horrible fracture in a football game his senior year. Then—what's now a common story—he got hooked on the painkillers he'd needed. When he ran out of doctors to prescribe them, he ended up on heroin.

"Last month he got caught trying to steal an iPod to buy dope. Minka's mother is an addiction therapist so she and I bailed Ben out of jail, got him into detox that night. Now he's in a new military style men's rehab called Recovery Strong.

"I told Ben about Andrea's surgery when I visited him and that her donor was a heroin addict. The next thing I knew Ben had gotten everyone in Recovery Strong to sign up with Michigan's Gift of Life as organ donors. These are copies of their registrations," she handed the papers to Dr. Korbuly. "And now those who still have driver's licenses—a lot have lost them—will get the red 'Donor' and little heart on them.

"Ben did tell me that just signing had put a little fear of God in them. They realized their organs could be next to go if they didn't stay clean."

Dr. Korbuly took the papers shaking his head, "This knocks me out. It will Dr. Rasmussen too. Actually the whole transplant team will be blown away. This has to be a national transplant first! Thank you, Maddie. Amazing!"

Then he looked at his watch and turned toward Andrea. "I'm sorry to break this up, but we need to do some final checks before Andrea's parents get here and she heads home to Chicago. Agnes, will you take Andrea to the clinic for me?"

"Assuming she doesn't run outside and kiss him goodbye," Agnes said standing up with Andrea and pointing out the window at the snowman.

"What a good idea, Mrs. Macbeth," Andrea said as she was being propelled toward the door. "Love you guys," she called over her shoulder. "See you in Chicago!"

Dr. Korbuly turned back to Minka and Maddie waving the sheaf of papers. "These will be the talk of the transplant floor for a long time. Please tell Ben the University of Michigan Transplant Center thanks the men of Recovery Strong. But we really hope we don't have to accept any of these offers."

Suddenly Andrea appeared back at the door, Agnes rolling her eyes behind her. Andrea tossed a navy plastic M Den bag at Maddie. "I almost forgot the shirt Dad got you. And now we're the three Ms and not just the M and Ms."

Maddie pulled the big block M shirt out of the bag and held it up to her chin. "A perfect fit, Andrea. Tell your dad I'll wear it to Chicago when we come."

"He will like that."

Then Andrea reached into her jacket pocket. "Just one more thing before we say goodbye, M." Andrea held up a water bottle with the impish grin Minka recognized. "I think we should ask these people who's better at our special trick."

"Winner winner chicken dinner you don't have a chance," Minka said picking up her own water bottle.

THE END

I'm indebted to Daniel, Rebecca, and Guiding Light, the men's strict recovery program in Grand Rapids, Michigan, for their contributions to this novel.

Joyce Jensen, a gifted Nurse Practitioner, wife, and mother who had a double lung transplant in 2014 at the University of Wisconsin Medical Center. While this novel is fiction, the letter below is not. Joyce wrote it to the 12-year-old boy whose tragic death saved Joyce's life.

No story I could ever make up about Gift of Life and the transplant experience can ever touch the power of this letter. It's not a coincidence that one of my two main (favorite) characters is twelve years old. This story is for Joshua and his family.

Dear Joshua,

It's been 5 years since you left this earth. This year you would've been 17, that's sometimes really hard to wrap my mind around. You missed so much yet I remain here because of you and your parents. I imagine you would be going into your senior year of high school. I think about all the firsts you have missed in the last 5 years; your first big Homecoming dance, your first kiss, your first time driving a car, and maybe your first job. I imagine you would be deciding your next step as you get ready to enter "adulthood"- what college should I attend? What career do I want? Where will life take me?

But you never got to ask those questions or experience those firsts. Your life was cut too short on that sunny crisp fall day 5 years ago in October. And that's when you came into my life and became a part of me...I will never forget that day. At just 12–years old, you breathed your last breath and then through a miracle you breathed life back into my failing tired body. That's remarkable Joshua. You saved me. Did you ever think in your short 12 years on this earth that you would save others? What a hero you are!

I will never take your lungs for granted, Joshua, I promise you that. It's really hard sometimes, Joshua, and some do not understand the magnitude of your gift-the gift of life. But I understand it and as we breathe together I will forever recognize you and your lungs allowing me to take a deep breath, to talk without gasping, and to live without struggling for air.

Your momma and family must be so sad without you, but I hope they will find a little peace knowing I'm working really hard to keep us going. I will honor your gift every day, every hour, every minute until we take our last breath together. I will help you experience things that you were unable to do in those 12 short years you were here on earth.

Do you know I have a celebration every year for you? It's a celebration of life, a time to celebrate our breathing together, and a time to give thanks. But within the celebration of surviving another year, I feel such sadness for you and your family. I know life is precious but still some do not understand that. Life isn't about rushing around, or worrying about every little detail, or stressing about work and extracurricular activities –t's about being present, appreciating your surroundings, loving one another, and living each day like it's your last. I get out of bed each day and thank God for what he has done for us and attempt to live life with a purpose-all because of you-a boy I've never met, a boy that didn't get to become a teenager or a man. A boy who didn't get to experience all of life's roller coaster ride of triumphs and devastation. A boy whose physical body is gone yet remains in me breathing in and out for me. A boy gone too soon.

Life is so precious, Joshua, and in an instant it can vanish. I guess that may sound cliche, but the reality is true and I want people to re-alize-don't sweat the small stuff, be grateful, be kind, and BREATHE! Thank you Joshua. Thank you to your mom, dad, and family that want nothing more than to hug you, talk to you, and be with you again. Let's keep doing life together, breathing in and out, in and out, in and out, in and out…

Made in the USA
Monee, IL
19 December 2020

54036176R10075